Chasing Thought

Thousand Eye Universe: Book 1

N E Riggs

N E Riggs
NRiggs0@gmail.com
NERiggs.com

FirstCityBooks.com

Editor: Emily Yetka emily.yetka@gmail.com

ISBN: 9798576546183

Let me tell you the story about the most important person in my life, a person I've never met.

Madrigan Farovan has never heard of me. We've never exchanged words, never seen each other. He saved my life, even if he doesn't know it.

It says more about me than about him that he's the most important person in my life. I don't have any people in my life. I could focus on strangers, but why bother? Madrigan is the one who matters, and so he's the one I follow.

I say that Madrigan's the only person in my life, but that's a lie. There's also Yonaven. I try not to think about Yonaven. Sometimes, I can avoid thinking about her for a long time. Yonaven has tried to stop me from following Madrigan, but she never succeeds for long. However many terrible things she's done, she can't bring herself to hurt me. She scolds me and yells at me and reasons with me and even begs me. As if I'd ever do what she wants me to do.

She tries, but it doesn't matter. It's Madrigan I care about. When he's asleep, I might notice other people, but that's the only time.

He saved my life. It's not much of a life that I have, but it's better than the alternative. If Madrigan knew, he'd come and save me again. I know he would. I know everything about him.

Since he saved my life, I want to return the favor. I can't do much, but I try. I'd do anything for Madrigan. For now, all I can do is tell his story.

1

Madrigan had never experienced silence. He wondered sometimes what it was like. Five years ago when he was newly free, he drank and took drugs, in an attempt to summon it. None of those things helped. They only made the world noisier.

In the end, the only choice was to learn to control his powers. There was still no silence, but Madrigan could at least muffle the thoughts that were always around him.

No matter how hard he practiced, there were certain thoughts that he couldn't keep out, couldn't ignore. Fear amplified mental voices better than anything, though anger and love made thoughts louder too. Over his life, Madrigan had learned to avoid certain places: hospitals, graveyards, police stations, prisons, wedding chapels, and sporting facilities. Ironically, the last was usually the worst, as most sentient species were stupidly invested in their team of choice.

Even when he avoided problematic places — which he couldn't always do — eventually, the thoughts and emotions of those around him caught up to him. Like now.

Screams filled the air, but they weren't as loud as the screams in Madrigan's head. He kept back, letting his associates take point. "Useless," Shorvin said as he rushed past Madrigan on short, stubby legs.

Madrigan's hands clenched into fists. He could feel

Shorvin's mind: such a weak, unfocused thing. One little push in the right place could kill him, or send him into a permanent vegetative state. Perhaps even better, a few little tweaks could alter his personality. Madrigan would love to have a slave, someone who fawned over him and took his whims as law.

"Focus!" Geffin's grip on his arm shook Madrigan out of his fantasy. He turned to see his best friend's face inches from his own, strained and covered in a thin layer of sweat.

"Sorry." Madrigan looked down the hallway. He didn't need a visual, but it helped. Four security guards huddled behind what little cover they could find: a desk turned on its side, a chair, and one another. They popped out just long enough to shoot their blasters, making Geffin's crew scatter. Other than Geffin and Madrigan, who stood at the far end of the hallway behind the door, no one had anywhere to hide.

If Madrigan didn't hurry, many people would die. The security guards would die; he and Geffin would ensure that. Madrigan wished more people on this terrible world would die, but they didn't have time for a bloodbath. He needed to focus, or else half of Geffin's crew might also die. He wouldn't mourn for Shorvin. If the Chaukee wasn't so damn useful, Madrigan would have already orchestrated his death. Shorvin being useful made no difference. Madrigan couldn't kill him, not by any means. Even if the situation looked completely natural, Geffin would know. He'd look at Madrigan with disappointment, and Madrigan couldn't handle that.

The second guard behind the desk had stars on the left breast of his uniform: an officer. Madrigan dropped into his mind.

The first few moments were the worst. The officer's fear buffeted him like strong waves in the ocean, ready to drown Madrigan at any moment. The crew had disabled communication down here, so the guards couldn't call for help. Possibilities flashed through the officer's mind, one on the heels of the previous, as he tried to think of a way for himself and the other three guards to survive.

With a smile, Madrigan wiped those thoughts away. The fear spiked in a wave greater than any other, so vast it threatened to encompass Madrigan. He angled himself and shot through it. He'd played with stronger minds than this, and he knew what to do.

Beyond the emotions waited the brain's sorting center. Human minds were easier to read than most. The consciousness couldn't sort through all the files waiting inside, but Madrigan could. It was as easy as looking up information on his jewel.

He sat in the chair in the center of a vast room. Books, files, and consoles surrounded him, going up and down as far as he could see. A lifetime of knowledge and experience waited here, most of the older parts buried under recent things. "Access security code for the basement of the treasury building," Madrigan said.

The books, files, and consoles around him spun and moved, looking for what he needed. They stopped after a second, a console pushing forward before him. A series of numbers and letters showed on it, as well as a note and a memory.

Madrigan stood from the chair. The mind rushed past him in reverse. The waves tried to take him again; they were stronger even than before. The sky showed an image of the outside world, which included the dead bodies of two of the other security guards.

This man knew he was going to die.

A sun hung dim over the turbulent ocean, clouds trying to obscure it. That was another manifestation of the man's fear. With a laugh, Madrigan reached for the sun. He gave a tug, and it came free from the sky.

The man wailed as he died.

Madrigan was expelled from the mind in time to see the last security guard turn to stare in shock as his superior fell over dead, seemingly without cause. His moment of distraction left him vulnerable. Three of Geffin's crew shot him, and he too died.

"I trust you got the code before you killed him," Geffin said to Madrigan, voice dry. "Unlike last time."

"I got it." Geffin didn't really mean it, but Madrigan still wanted to flinch at the reminder. He'd been justified in his distraction last time, but it was still no excuse. He was supposed to be one of the most powerful saireishi alive. He needed to start acting like it. "You need his hand and his eyes." Madrigan pointed at the officer.

"Take him to the scanner."

At Geffin's command, four of the crew hurried forward. They hoisted up the officer, pulling him to the door at the end of the hallway. One placed the officer's hand on the scanner while another forced his glassy eyes open.

Madrigan repeated the string of letters and numbers, which a third crew member typed into the pad beside the scanner. The Hreckin officials thought that this system would be more secure. 'Jewels are easy to hack,' they told one another while the officer watched on. 'Something more primitive might be better. Our DNA and retina scans, combined with a long code that only a few people know, will keep out any thieves.' Though Madrigan hadn't looked for it, the memory had been prominent in the officer's memory, next to the code.

With a soft ping, the door opened. The officer's body was tossed outside as the crew streamed inside. "Take whatever you can easily grab. We have two hundred seconds," Geffin called as they swarmed over the treasure within. He strolled toward the door with Madrigan, the two of them the last ones inside.

"Maybe the historical section of the treasury wasn't the best place," Madrigan said as he looked around inside. Wide, narrow boxes held paintings. Statues, some with bits missing, clogged one side of the vault. Those were all too big to take — and too hard to sell.

The crew members found some containers with gems and jewelry, which they happily smashed. In seconds, their pockets bulged, but they kept going, taking as much as they could.

"Ten seconds," Geffin said, tapping his jewel. "Move, people!"

Most of the crew snatched one or three last items, then left the room. The group continued down the hall back the way they came, stepping over or around the corpses of the security guards. Geffin and Madrigan stayed near the center of the group, Geffin so everyone could hear his orders, and Madrigan for protection.

All the security systems were still down. They were all primitive and pathetically easy for Madrigan to hack or just shut down. Only stupid, horrible people lived on Hreckin. That was why they came here. Horrible people deserved to be killed and robbed, and it was easier against stupid people.

The crew made it out of the building. The security guards at the main gate slept. Madrigan checked their minds to be sure. They wouldn't wake for a few more hours. The robots, which were so old they barely counted as such, had been shut down by the guards.

Their spaceship was parked two blocks from the treasury. Geffin had complained about this while planning the raid, wishing they could get the *Otteran* closer. There were no flat spaces big enough for a frigate that size, not that were closer. Madrigan promised Geffin that he'd give the crew enough time to land, make the hit, and then get out.

Three of the crew had stayed behind with the ship. The *Otteran*'s engines hummed to life as the crew reached the park where they had left the frigate. The door opened and the ramp lowered at their approach. As soon as the last person was inside, the ramp retracted, the door closed, and the ship lifted into the air.

Madrigan sank into an empty seat at the rear of the cockpit and closed his eyes. This was the hardest part of the plan. The further away a person was, the harder they were to reach.

A com channel opened. "*Otteran*, we don't have records of the purpose of your visit," a bored, male voice said. "You only landed an hour ago. Is something wrong?"

Bored people were easier than wary people. Madrigan flung his thoughts towards the planet, searching for the person on the other end. A few miles from the treasury building at the space communication center, he found the man. He'd been working for hours, had less than two left until the end of his shift. Despite copious amounts of coffee and a few stims that he took when his supervisor wasn't looking, he was exhausted. The man wasn't bored, just tired.

That worked just as well for Madrigan. He reached into the man's mind and stirred the waters. The exhaustion swelled, drenching everything.

"We got a sudden call from back home," Bakigan, the pilot of the *Otteran*, said. "We have to leave. Sorry."

The man yawned, loudly enough that everyone in the cockpit heard it. "What's your destination?"

The *Otteran* was well away from the planet by now, and its weapons. As a new world that had a liking for primitive methods, Hreckin had only one weapon satellite in orbit around it, which was on the opposite side of the planet at the moment. Even if anyone down there became suspicious before the *Otteran* jumped into hyperspace — though Madrigan was working to prevent that from happening — probably no attack would come in time to stop them.

Geffin leaned in front of Bakigan to speak over the com. "Waljik 6," he said.

The man on the other end yawned again, louder this time. "Have a safe trip and come back soon." The com channel closed.

Bakigan let out a whoop as his antennae twitched over his head. Geffin didn't relax until the frigate made the jump into hyperspace.

With a soft gasp, Madrigan slumped back in his chair. From space, it was harder to hear people on the planet, unless he made an effort. In hyperspace, he could only touch the minds of those with him on the same ship. Perhaps if another ship flew close enough, he could hear the thoughts of those on the other ship, but Madrigan had never been able to test that.

It wasn't quiet, but it was as close as he ever got.

Sometimes, Madrigan thought he would like to spend most of his life in hyperspace, with a handful of people on the same ship and no one else. It would be lonely, but he'd like a few months of loneliness.

"Well done," Geffin told the crew as he, Madrigan, and Bakigan joined the rest of the crew in the large common area. The *Otteran* was small for a frigate, but it easily held all fifty crew members. When the rest of the crew didn't move, Geffin waved at their stuffed pockets. "Empty them out. You know the rules. Everyone shares equally." Bakigan nodded emphatically. If he hadn't been guaranteed part of the haul, he wouldn't have stayed aboard the *Otteran*. Without him, the escape would have been much harder.

Madrigan left the common area. Geffin didn't need his help for this. Most of the crew were criminals, but they obeyed Geffin. No one would try to hide any of the treasure away.

Crew quarters lined the lower deck, across from the large hold. A common refresher stood at each end. The quarters each had two bunks and two closets, and no more. It wasn't luxurious living by any standards, but Madrigan didn't mind. He'd lived in worse places. Here, he only had to share with Geffin. Here, no cameras watched him as he slept. Here, no one tortured him under the guise of training.

He stopped at his quarters long enough to grab a change of clothes and toiletries then headed to the nearest refresher. Hot water cascaded down on him, taking away the grime and blood. On days like this, when Madrigan had to touch many minds, he always needed a shower. Even after all these years, touching a stranger's mind made him feel dirty.

He looked even paler with soap all over him. Madrigan closed his eyes and scrubbed harder.

At least he knew better than to get distracted once inside a stranger's mind. The people on Hreckin were all horrible people. He shuddered at what thoughts he might have encountered if he'd allowed himself to wander. He'd touched such thoughts before, and wanted nothing more than to avoid such people in the future.

Every member of the *Otteran* crew was scum. Most had criminal records. The others only lacked records because the Neutral and Gray law enforcement agencies hadn't caught up with them yet. They were still better than the kindest and most generous people on Hreckin.

After two minutes, the hot water shut off. The ship didn't allow more than that, not even to Madrigan or Geffin. Neutral police would be after them soon — if they were unlucky, the Gray police might join in. As such, hey couldn't afford to waste ship resources.

Hot air switched on, drying Madrigan. He stepped out of

the narrow space and pulled on fresh clothes. Finally, he felt sentient again.

A few other crew members came over as he left the refresher. Most of them waved or thanked him for helping. Madrigan couldn't help but grin back. Why had he ever thought to live with law-abiding citizens? These people were so much better. They never judged him.

Geffin was back at their quarters. A small stack of gems and jewelry waited on Geffin's bunk, another the same size waited on Madrigan's.

Madrigan groaned. "I told you, I don't need any treasure." He closed the door behind him so the rest of the crew wouldn't hear them argue.

"And I told you, it will look weird if you don't take anything. You want the crew to know our real plan?" Geffin waved a hand to encompass everything. "That happens, and we won't have a crew."

They'd had this argument every day for months, ever since they first conceived their plan. Madrigan was too tired to keep it up today. When Geffin next went to bed, Madrigan could stuff his share of the treasure into Geffin's bag. If he tweaked Geffin's mind, the other man wouldn't notice.

Though he'd entertained that thought more than once, it still made him want to squirm. He hadn't mentioned it to Geffin. He hadn't mentioned anything involving him touching Geffin's mind. Madrigan's powers made other people nervous at best, dangerous at worst. Geffin was the only person he'd ever met who didn't seem to care.

Was that because Geffin didn't think Madrigan would peek into his mind? Madrigan hadn't, not even once. Some of Geffin's louder thoughts came through to him — he couldn't do anything to stop those. That was all he'd ever heard.

If I look into Geffin's mind, we won't be friends anymore. That thought came to him within hours of their first meeting, and it hadn't left him since. It was his own thought. Madrigan could never mistake his thoughts for anyone else's. Despite that, or perhaps because of that, it festered.

Maybe if he'd looked into Geffin's mind during the early days of their friendship, they could have moved past it. Now it was a huge thing to Madrigan, and it terrified him.

He could never look into the other man's mind. Not to confirm details about a heist, not to trick him into taking Madrigan's share of the treasure, and certainly not to confirm how he really felt about Madrigan. That last part never ended well. Madrigan knew that many times over.

"How long 'til we reach Waljik 6?" He dropped the treasure into his suitcase, pressing it between pieces of underwear. While it was in his suitcase, he didn't have to think about it.

Geffin tapped his jewel. "Just under four hours. You going to take a nap?"

"I should." Four hours was just enough time to make him more tired when he woke up. The sleep would refresh his mind if not his body, and his mind was the far more important of the two. Madrigan climbed onto his narrow bunk, pulling the blanket around him. "We're sure this is going to work, aren't we?"

Geffin snorted. "You mean *you're* sure this is going to work. Because this was your idea. I was fine just stealing and killing."

"You thought of it first."

"Doesn't mean anything. I think of lots of plans. There's a reason I don't use most of my ideas. This is as close to being Light as I can get, and it's all your fault."

Madrigan turned his head to the wall so Geffin wouldn't see his smile. "I'm good at corrupting people."

"Well, we'll be able to kill more people before we're done, so I won't complain. I'll wake you up a few minutes before we drop out of hyperspace."

"Thanks."

Being a saireishi had a few advantages. One was that it never took long to fall asleep. Madrigan reached into his own mind and pressed in the right spot. A second advantage of going to sleep that way was that it kept away the nightmares. Ever since learning the trick, Madrigan never went to sleep the normal way.

He drifted off with a smile, eager, for the first time in far too long, for the future.

2

Illusions and holograms danced through the air, one indistinguishable from the other. Vilstair pressed her lips together and ignored them all, running as fast as she could.

Colored lights swirled in front of her, momentarily obscuring her vision. "Fucking—" Vilstair ran into the wall they had concealed. "You're only making things worse for yourself!"

"I disagree, Officer." Globlan's voice came tinny through the hallway but clear enough for her to hear his smug tone.

Vilstair pushed off the wall, rubbing her sore nose. It was flat, which was the only thing that had saved it from being crushed or broken, but it still hurt. Once again, she blessed her mixed genetics.

She continued down the hallway, forcing herself to move at a slower pace. The Gray gods knew what the next set of holograms and illusions might disguise. Damn it, she needed a partner. She ignored the pang that shot through her at the memory of Writhim. His death wouldn't be in vain.

A few more steps and she reached an intersection. Riotous colors showed in every direction, offering her no help. The colors combined with her green skin to make an awful color. Annoying music now played, all the awful songs that children of all species seemed to love.

Vilstair tapped the jewel connected to her temple. A diagram of the building filtered over her vision, though even that wasn't enough to display all of Globlan's stupid tricks. An exit waited to the left. Right and straight would take her deeper into the building, through different sections.

Damn it, Globlan could be anywhere in the building. She tapped her jewel again, switching to a heat sensor overlay. That didn't help. There were dozens of people inside the building, all wandering about. What sort of criminal built his lair in a fun park? Without the amusement park, he wouldn't have access to the holograms. And the fun park was what brought all the saireishi here.

"Fuck you," Vilstair told the ceiling, knowing Globlan would hear her through the speakers.

"Should you be using that sort of language, Officer? You're Gray."

He knew she was coming. He couldn't stay here, not unless he wanted to get captured. There must be something he had planned, some way to escape. Local police surrounded the amusement park, checking everyone who left. Globlan had drugged the saireishi into giving him these illusions. As long as they stayed psychotropic, the saireishi couldn't concentrate enough to get him out. And as soon as they came down from their high, they'd turn on him. That was worse than getting captured by her or the local police.

She headed straight. It seemed as good an option as any. As she jogged, she tugged her lower lip into her mouth. It stretched further than a human's would, though not as far as a Parleni's. Vilstair was a mix between the two. When she lifted her hand, the webbing between her fingers looked thicker than usual. Another illusion? Or just the colors and holograms making her look awful? Surely, the saireishi should concentrate on something else. She wasn't going to stop because of something as small as that.

Other than that, she saw only distant holograms and illusions as she walked. Had Globlan lost track of her? Or maybe the saireishi were beginning to sober up. She didn't care why, and broke into a sprint again.

When she reached the next intersection, colors rained down on her, so fast and thick that she couldn't see anything through them. Vilstair pressed herself against the wall, swearing. Though she tapped her jewel many times, even that didn't help. It could penetrate the holograms, but not the illusions. Those bypassed her technology, sinking directly into her brain.

Mind tricks weren't supposed to work as well against her, thanks to her mixed genetics. That was part of why Yafan sent her and Writhim here. Being an Ill-gotten hadn't helped Writhim when the illusions made him walk into a turbine he couldn't see. Being Ill-gotten didn't help Vilstair now.

The saireishi must have found a way around her unusual brain chemistry. Or maybe, when enough saireishi were working together, brain composition didn't matter as much.

Vilstair continued forward. She glared at the colors around her, resenting them. She wanted to rub her eyes, but she knew that wouldn't help. That might make the holograms disappear, but it would do nothing for the illusions. Those were in her mind.

Maybe that wouldn't fix her problem, but would it hurt? Vilstair closed her eyes. Since she could barely see anyway, she might as well. To her surprise, all the colors dissipated, leaving only black. Didn't sairei affect the mind? Since it was an illusion, perhaps it affected the part of her mind that controlled what she saw.

She still couldn't see, but now she was less annoyed.

With one hand stretched out in front of her, she waded forward. Like this, she could only inch ahead. If she took so long that Globlan escaped, there was no point in doing this.

She tapped her jewel. Though the jewel interfaced directly with her mind, it was meant to supplement her senses, not replace them. Though she could see a diagram of the building and her approximate location within it, that didn't help much. There was a wall somewhere ahead of her, but she couldn't tell how far. Knowing it was there made her walk all the slower.

A few more taps of the jewel offered no assistance. If she had a jewel that included advanced navigational systems, she could have walked through the building blind. She didn't have that. Her superiors judged that heat sensors and infrared were enough — those were already more than most people had on their jewels.

"Should have been born blind." She wouldn't have survived until birth in that case. She was Ill-gotten: she'd been conceived and grown in a laboratory. Ill-gotten children with deficiencies were thrown out before they reached maturity.

An echo came, distant. Vilstair stopped and tilted her head to the side. It came from the right. According to the diagram from her jewel, a large room waited in that direction, used for storage. With a mental shrug, she headed that way.

After a few timid steps, her hand found the wall. This gave her the courage to walk faster since she had some idea of where she was. Another tap of her jewel zoomed in on the diagram. She hadn't walked into a wall yet: that gave her a sense of the scale.

Another noise came, closer this time. It wasn't Globlan, taunting her over the building's communication system. Speaking of, why hadn't he bothered her recently? He'd probably already fled the building, looking for a way to escape the fun park. Vilstair broke into a jog.

The wall fell abruptly away as the overlay suggested she should have walked into a wall. When she waved her hand to the side, she smacked it against a door. She must be inside the storage room.

Despite knowing she shouldn't, Vilstair opened her eyes. For the first time in far too long, she saw the world around her. A few lights blinked along the ceiling of the room, providing inadequate illumination. Crates lined one side of the room, broken equipment the other. Everything was covered in dust and cobwebs.

It was smaller than it should be. Vilstair compared what she could see versus the diagram — the room should have been four times that size, not the cramped space she could see.

Another illusion? A far more subtle one this time? With all those drugs in their bodies, could the saireishi form something this detailed? Maybe it was a hologram.

A noise came again, closer. It bounced off the ceiling though it seemed to come from beyond the wall. Vilstair swung an arm at the closest crate. Her hand struck nothing but air.

Hologram or illusion: it didn't matter. The crates and equipment weren't real. Vilstair strode forward, squeezing her eyes shut once more. It should have taken one step before she ran into something, but she kept going. Two, three, four steps. On the fifth, her shin banged into something hard.

"Fucking hells—" Vilstair opened her eyes again.

The room looked different. The poor lighting was the same, as were the dust and cobwebs. There were crates and equipment off to the side, far away. The room finally looked like the size it ought to be.

More importantly, Vilstair could now see a dozen people sprawled on the floor in a loose circle, most of them children. They leaned against one another, muttering and laughing. It reminded Vilstair of that night she had during the academy when she and some other recruits got into the good painkillers. The morning after had been a bitch, but the night itself had been brilliant. Thanks to the recording another recruit made, Vilstair had seen that same stupid, vacant look on her own face.

Globlan had snatched twelve saireishi during their vacation: two teachers and ten children. These must be them.

Vilstair crouched beside the nearest adult, a Huckfering male with graying fur. She poked his shoulder to ensure that he was real. Her finger touched coarse fur, and Vilstair sighed. Then she gripped both his shoulders and gave him a firm shaking.

"Whoa." The Huckfering blinked open his eyes. His whiskers twitched, and his sharp ears perked up. "Hey, sister. You look awesome!"

"Sober up!" Vilstair smacked him across his long nose.

His head snapped to the side. For a moment, he gaped, rubbing his cheek. Then he laughed and slid backward.

"Don't you dare! I need you coherent!"

She didn't know what Globlan had given them. Whatever it was, it was still affecting the saireishi. When she stared at the nearest child, she frowned. Both adults were giggling, but the children barely moved. Children required different doses of medicine than adults. Something that made an adult high could kill a child.

She kept one hand gripping the Huckfering while she shoved the other hand deep into one of her jacket pockets. As a Gray operative, she carried a few painkillers at all times. Even injured, she was still expected to carry out her duty. Because the painkillers messed with the mind, she also had a sobriety pill. It had been tailored to her biology, which was unique. Well, Huckfering were among the more robust species in the galaxy. Hopefully, it wouldn't hurt him.

"Don't want it," the Huckfering said when she tried to shove the pill into his mouth.

"Tough shit." Vilstair gripped his face and his jaw, pressed his mouth shut until he swallowed. Then she sat back and waited. The pill shouldn't take long.

Within thirty seconds, the Huckfering began shaking. It started as little twitches, then grew into full body spasms. Vilstair thanked the Gray gods that she hadn't given the pill to one of the children. She shoved her arm under his head to act as a pillow, so he wouldn't give himself a concussion.

He muttered throughout, words Vilstair couldn't decipher. Suddenly he sat up, eyes wide. "The shit?"

"Welcome back to reality, where we all miss drugs. You need to stop the illusions, help your fellow saireishi, and tell me where to find Globlan."

For a moment, the Huckfering only stared at her. When his gaze fell to her jacket, his eyes narrowed. "You're a Gray operative?"

"Vilstair Bila of the Gray interstellar police."

"Excellent. Thank you for your help, Officer Bila. I'll take care of things here. You find Globlan."

"Where is he?"

The Huckfering's eyes went distant. He tapped the jewel at his temple, and a beep sounded from Vilstair's. Standing this close, they didn't need to know each other to share information. A location appeared before her eyes. A blinking red dot moved away from this building, heading towards the far side of the fun park. It moved slowly, so Globlan must be on foot.

"Thank you."

The Huckfering nodded. "Just get him. Kidnapping and drugging saireishi is a galaxy-wide offense. Especially when it involves children."

Vilstair clapped him on the upper arm and hurried out of the room. She could see clearly now. Though wonderful, it took her a moment to adjust. Then she shook her head and broke into a sprint.

As she ran, she tapped her jewel. "This is where you can

find the saireishi," she told the local authorities. "The children need medical attention."

"Understood, Officer. We're on our way. Do you know where Globlan is?"

"I'm getting closer to his location." Vilstair didn't transmit his location. The Huckfering must have connected her to his jewel unless saireishi had some other tracking method that could be connected to a jewel. Globlan was armed and dangerous, and Vilstair wanted to catch him herself. "Head to the north side of the park." However angry she was, she wanted backup in case she needed it. Writhim should have been her backup, but he was gone now.

She ignored the pang in her chest. Now wasn't the time to mourn. She ran faster.

With no holograms distracting or confusing her and the diagram showing her the way, Vilstair quickly exited the building and turned north. When she entered the building less than an hour ago, plenty of people were still wandering around the amusement park. Now she saw only security. A man who captured and drugged saireishi was capable of anything, so the local authorities had gotten the civilians out of the way.

None of the security stopped Vilstair though two ran after her. They knew who she was and who she was chasing. As she approached the blinking red light, Vilstair checked that her blaster was on stun mode. She wanted Globlan alive, so he could spend years making up for his crimes. When he died, he could then continue to pay.

A concession house stood between her and Globlan. Vilstair slowed as she rounded it, not wanting to give her position away. She reached the edge and poked her head out, ready to fire. There was no one there.

Frowning, she checked the tracker the Huckfering gave her. The blinking red light was right here. Globlan should be standing in front of her.

What if the Huckfering had made a mistake? Or what if he was a liar, on Globlan's side and trying to send her the wrong way? Damn it, she hadn't even thought of that.

She reached for her jewel when the blinking red light grew smaller. How could it be smaller? From the speed, Globlan still wasn't in a ship.

When she glanced around the area, she gasped. A manhole covered the entrance to the sewers. Of course.

A stun shot from her blaster made the cover spring out of the hole, where it rolled to one side. A noise came from within, echoing oddly but sounding dismayed. Vilstair hoped Globlan was dismayed.

She approached the open hole from the side, keeping low and pointing her blaster inside. Thanks to the infrared on her jewel, she could see something large and hot moving around down there. It was about the size of most humanoids, and it was quickly moving away.

Not quickly enough though. Vilstair stunned it. The figure slumped to the side and didn't move.

A quick scan showed nothing else alive in the vicinity — or at least nothing big and alive. Vilstair climbed down the ladder on the side. The rungs were slippery, but that didn't bother her. She could grip wet things more easily than most sentients, her webbed skin sticking to the rungs.

When she was near the bottom, she scanned the area again. Still nothing but the person she stunned. The figure lay a few feet from the ladder, their face resting on the edge of a puddle. Vilstair used her foot to push the person over onto their back. In the dark of the sewers, she couldn't see, but her jewel could still scan the face and DNA. It was Globlan.

"Let's see how much you enjoy a lifetime in prison." Vilstair smirked even though he couldn't hear her. She'd gotten him, and that was what mattered.

By the time Vilstair got Globlan's bulk up the ladder and out of the sewer, the local police had arrived. A Drilthin man and a Jrikshon man, both bulging with muscles, took Globlan from her, hoisting him up into a waiting police hovervan.

Vilstair shook hands with the local sheriff. "We'll transport the prisoner to Capitania," he said after thanking her.

"Capitania?" She blinked.

He spread his claws wide. "His crime was against saireishi. Where else can he be tried?"

Vilstair made a soft noise under her breath but didn't argue. She wanted him to stand trial on Diresi. He'd killed a Gray operative. But he'd also kidnapped saireishi and threatened the lives of the children in the group. These saireishi were Unattached, and so crimes against them could only be tried on Capitania. She shouldn't complain. Whatever punishment Globlan got would be worse on Capitania than it would be on Diresi.

Writhim would have to be satisfied with that.

She copied her contact information to the sheriff so that he could, in turn, give that to the officials on Capitania. If they needed Vilstair present for the trial, they would call her. She doubted they'd need her. The word of a saireishi would be more than enough to convict Globlan.

"How are the saireishi?"

"They'll live. They're already heading back to Capitania. Some of the children need advanced medical attention." The sheriff shrugged.

"I want to know what happens to them. Pass that on with my information."

"Will do. Anything else you need, Officer? The, er, remains of your partner—"

Vilstair grimaced. There wasn't much left of Writhim.

The saireishi had made him walk into a turbine he hadn't realized was there. "I don't need to take them — er, him — home. But thank you." Before he could ask for her help in cleaning up, she left.

One of the police hovervans flew her back to her ship, which she had left near the amusement park entrance. She thanked the police for the lift and got into the *Nebula's Edge*. Once inside, she sighed and slumped in the pilot's chair. Gray gods, she hoped she never got another mission like this one.

A tap of her jewel opened a com channel to Gray HQ on Diresi. Yafan answered, leaning close. "What happened?" he asked, ears pressed against the side of his head. He already knew about Writhim's death.

Vilstair gave a short report of the last few hours. Yafan made vague noises as he recorded her report then asked for a few details. It was all standard stuff, things Vilstair could do in her sleep. "I didn't argue that Globlan should be taken to Capitania," she said at the end.

"Nor should you." Yafan shook his head, his whiskers stiff with disapproval. "Messing with saireishi. What in the hells was he thinking? Our representatives on Capitania will make sure he sees justice, Vilstair, don't worry. The galactic senate ensures that anyone who messes with Unattached saireishi ends up regretting it. Writhim can be at peace."

"Yeah. About that. There isn't enough of him to bring home."

Yafan coughed, his ears twitching violently. "Gray gods. I had wondered why you didn't mention the body. I'll contact his family. They'll want to make arrangements for a funeral. You don't have to be here for it."

She'd never met Writhim's family. He hadn't been close to them, and she had only met him a month ago. "I'll be there," she said, because they deserved to hear the details from her. It was also a chance to say goodbye to Writhim, and she needed that. "Do you want me to head back now?"

He checked something on a screen she couldn't see. "No. Stay there a little longer. The saireishi have left, but Globlan hasn't been transported yet. I want you nearby in case he left us more surprises. Keep in contact." He raised a paw in farewell then cut the connection.

So much for getting out of here. Vilstair slid lower in her seat, her knees banging against the console.

Like most Neutral worlds, the authorities on Rollaron didn't move quickly. Neutrals loved paperwork and checking protocols and every other stupid little thing that took too long. After an hour, the sheriff called Vilstair to get her report. She copied him the official one she gave to Yafan, then, at the sheriff's request, sent a second copy to Capitania.

After that, she had to wait some more. When another hour passed and she heard nothing new, she left the cockpit to head further back into her cruiser. Like most police operatives, she spent more time on her ship than any one planet. The *Nebula's Edge* had everything she needed to make it a home. Three bunks folded out from the wall, one above the other. A couch sat in front of a large console, and the refresher was larger than those on most cruisers.

Vilstair grimaced when she opened Writhim's locker. His clothes stared back at her, accusing. She found a box that she dumped them into, praying that Yafan would call with a mission. Anything was better than this.

If she was already dreading the funeral, did that make her a horrible partner and friend? Probably. But it didn't change how she felt.

When a ping came from her jewel an hour later, Vilstair sighed. "Thank all the Gray gods." She left the box half-packed as she walked into the cockpit, tapping her jewel. Yafan's image appeared on the display, even more haggard than before. "Did something happen to the saireishi?"

"No. We've got a crisis on Hreckin. Thieves hit a government building, killed at least four people. You're the only operative nearby. Can you take it? I know you've got—"

"Yes," Vilstair said, hating herself. Yafan looked hopeful as she settled into her chair, pulling the restraints around her. "Don't worry about it. I'll take point on this. When you get someone else, I can go home. That won't take more than a day or so, will it?" The *Nebula's Edge* rose from the ground as she hit buttons.

"That should be more than enough time for someone else to take over. Thanks, Vilstair."

"No problem. I'll call you when I get there." She hung up then connected with the local authorities to explain why she had to leave. They didn't like it, but they assured her that they would transport Globlan to Capitania. Vilstair thanked them for their understanding.

By the time the conversation had ended, the *Nebula's Edge* was far away from Rollaron, perpendicular to the orbits of most of the planets. Far enough away to safely make the jump into hyperspace. Vilstair checked that the computer had the correct coordinates for Hreckin, then pulled the lever.

The stars changed from pinpoints to lines as she left real space. For the next four hours, which was how long it would take to reach Hreckin, she couldn't communicate with anyone. Which meant she wouldn't have to explain Writhim's death to his family yet.

She was definitely a coward. For the moment, she didn't care.

3

A hand on his arm brought Madrigan awake. He could sleep long and deep while still being aware. So long as part of his mind remained aware, it would watch his surroundings while he rested. While he could give nightmare-free rest to himself, he hadn't learned to share that with other people.

"We're almost at Waljik 6," Geffin said, taking his hand back. "I'll be in the cockpit."

"You could wait for me," Madrigan said, but Geffin was already gone from their quarters. He shook his head but smiled. Geffin's impatience was nothing new.

He tugged on his boots, having otherwise slept fully dressed. Patting his thin hair into place, he hurried to the cockpit.

Most of the crew was awake. They waved or called out as he passed. "No one on Waljik 6 will arrest us, right?" asked Polf. Before Geffin broke them out of prison, they'd been serving three life sentences. The Neutral and Gray police would love to get them behind bars again.

"Don't worry, we'll be fine." Madrigan gave them a quick smile.

Only Geffin and Bakigan were in the cockpit when Madrigan arrived. Numbers counted down on the display, quickly approaching zero. When the numbers hit zero, Bakigan pulled a lever to drop them out of hyperspace. The lines outside the window crashed to a halt and turned into dots of light, stars scattered far away.

This area of space had only been recently explored, the oldest settlements three hundred years old. Many were far newer. At one hundred fifty, Hreckin was average for this area.

As civilization expanded into this area, space stations came with. They provided stopping-off points, places to buy supplies, and a chance to contact the rest of the galaxy. There were ten Waljik stations, all built along the same lines. When exploration moved even further into the unknown regions, Waljik 6 no longer functioned as it once did. Instead of pioneers and rebels and dreamers and scientists, it housed smugglers and ne'er-do-wells and other scum. It was the sort of place where the crew of the *Otteran* wouldn't stick out.

It was also an excellent place to sell some of their treasure. Gems could be easily transported and sold anywhere, as they were hard to trace. Jewelry less so. If the crew wanted to turn the jewelry into money, they needed to find a seller, someone who didn't care about its origin.

Geffin knew such a being, a man whose business spread across the ten Waljik stations and beyond. They had contacted him before hitting the treasury building on Hreckin, and so the man should be waiting for them.

A com channel opened from the station when the *Otteran* exited hyperspace. "Registration and purpose of visit."

Bakigan leaned forward as he spoke since some people had trouble understanding him. "This is the *Otteran*, here for business and pleasure. We plan to stay two or three standard days."

"You can bring a shuttle to the designated landing bay." A close-up of the station appeared on the display, a hangar on the near side marked. "Obey all station rules during your stay, or you will be handed over to the Gray interstellar police. Have a nice stay."

"You too, asshole," Bakigan said after the com channel shut down, snapping his beak for emphasis. He glanced at Geffin. "You sure about this? We've got an alternative registration."

Geffin shook his head. "Not yet. When we go to Thlist, we go as the *Oranteran*. For now, we're the *Otteran*."

Bakigan sighed as he maneuvered the ship into an orbit high over the station. "If you say so, boss. I like not being me."

"Don't worry so much. Madrigan and I know what we're doing." When Bakigan didn't lose his grumpy expression, Geffin laughed and clapped him on the shoulder. Then he and Madrigan left the cockpit.

Six crew members waited near the shuttle. It wouldn't hold more than ten people. "Remember to keep your weapons on stun mode," Geffin said as he, Madrigan, and the other six took their seats on the shuttle. "I don't want any trouble while we're on Waljik 6. Well, no unexpected trouble." He grinned at that, winking at Madrigan.

Because the gods hated Madrigan, one of the crew on the shuttle was Shorvin. He took the seat behind Madrigan's, leaning forward so that his breath tickled the back of Madrigan's neck. "I've got a contact here, boss. Can I meet her?"

Even without his power, Madrigan didn't need to know what Shorvin meant by contact. The man's leer gave it away. "We're supposed to stay together," he said.

Shorvin ignored him, never looking away from Geffin. "You can come too if you like. She's got business associates."

"I doubt we'll have time for that," Geffin said. "Stick with us, Shorvin. If you leave, you know what will happen."

Though Geffin had been the one to say the threat, Shorvin glared at Madrigan. Everyone knew who enforced Geffin's threats. It wasn't how Madrigan wanted to deal with the rest of the crew. Except with Shorvin, he didn't have to.

He glared back at the man. "Don't think I won't notice."

"I think you like to watch. Pervert." Shorvin sat back in his seat and stopped talking, at least.

Madrigan wanted to rub his brow, to soothe away his headache. That would only trouble the other crew members. They got nervous when he reached for his head, no matter how banal the reason. He didn't need to touch his head to use his power. In holocins, that was what actors did when pretending to be saireishi. It didn't matter how many times Madrigan had explained this to others, they didn't believe it. He soon stopped trying to explain. He had better ways to spend his time than complaining over misrepresentation from the holocin industry.

The trip from the *Otteran* to the station took only a few minutes. They berthed the shuttle in the indicated dock. Many other shuttles filled the bay, along with cruisers and a battered Faranis-fighter. Madrigan let Geffin and the others go on ahead of him, which gave him a few moments to massage his temples.

A small robot had been on the shuttle with them. Madrigan told it to watch the shuttle but left the shuttle otherwise unlocked. He always assumed that he might need to leave in a hurry. He then checked that his spare jewel was inside the refresher, lying in the middle on the floor. With that done, he walked quickly to catch up with the others.

Shorvin noticed him coming from behind, and smirked at him. The headache returned, and Madrigan fought not to grind his teeth. Gods, he hated that man.

Geffin's contact wanted to meet in the bowels of the station. Though plenty of shady and out-right illegal dealings went on at all the Waljik stations, Geffin remained paranoid. After three prison sentences — all of which he'd escaped from within a year or three — Geffin worried about being caught.

"I know I've got you now," he told Madrigan whilst they planned, "but I don't fancy going back. I won't be sent to a Neutral prison if I'm caught again. It'll be a Gray one, probably on Diresi."

As they headed deeper into the station, Geffin called his contact. "Immediately?" Geffin said, stopping so fast one of the other crew members almost walked into him. He was silent for a moment, listening. The scowl grew deeper. "Yes, well, I appreciate your diligence. It saves me time. We're headed there now. Bye."

"They know we were coming, boss?" Polf asked, snout twitching. A family walked past, and they glared at them. Geffin was paranoid, but Polf suspected everyone, even children. A week ago, Madrigan offered to look into their mind, have a rummage round and maybe fix some of their obvious issues, but Polf refused. They refused nicely since Madrigan and Geffin were the only people they trusted. Because Polf trusted him, Madrigan couldn't fix them without permission. Until Polf, he hadn't realized how frustrating that could be.

"He detected the *Otteran* the moment we came out of hyperspace. He's been monitoring us." Geffin clenched his fists. "I said we might have merchandise to discuss in a few days. Why in the hells has he been tracking me?"

Polk gripped their blaster and grinned. "You want us to take care of him? You've got other contacts."

Geffin sighed. "We can't attack him. That will atttract attention we don't need from the station security. Besides, attacking your suppliers is bad business. No, *we* can't attack him." As he said this, Geffin looked right at Madrigan, as if Madrigan needed such a pointed look to understand his meaning.

"I'll take care of it," Madrigan said.

With a laugh, Polk poked him in the side with their

elbow. "We're damn lucky to have you. How'd you become an unregistered saireishi, anyway? I thought that was impossible."

"Come on, I don't want to linger," Geffin said before Madrigan had to answer.

The group picked up their pace, or as much as they could while in the marketplace. People were clustered in here thick as they passed wilting fruit. Madrigan stared at that. Fresh produce cost far too much on space stations. He hadn't realized there was anyone rich enough to afford that on Waljik 6. He would have to pay closer attention, lest someone take him by surprise.

He walked near the back of the group. Not at the very rear, because then people would assume he was one of Geffin's guards. When they met others, Madrigan played Geffin's accountant. A few months back, Madrigan met an accountant who knew some interesting loopholes. Thanks to what he learned from the man — without his knowledge, of course — Madrigan would never have to pay more than point-one percent tax again. He was still implementing the investment schemes, but he would never have to work again.

Not that he had to work now. If Madrigan ever needed money, he found someone rich and twisted their mind. They happily transferred to him as much money as he wanted. He didn't take enough to ruin their lives, and he never did that to anyone who truly needed money.

"You're a rogue for the poor," Geffin said the first time he saw Madrigan do that. "I can appreciate that. Want to put your talents to better use and really screw over the rich?"

Geffin was his only friend, so Madrigan would have said yes regardless. Still, he liked the idea of being a crusader, of helping the galaxy to be a better place.

As they walked through the marketplace, a few people got close, and one young woman tried to pickpocket Polk.

Polk grabbed her hand and twisted her wrist, nearly hard enough to break it. She ran off, whimpering. No one had any ill intentions towards them. Madrigan didn't have to listen very hard to pick up things like that. Cruelty was a song he knew far too well.

Once past the last stall, they were able to walk easier. Madrigan felt eyes on them. He didn't look around; he didn't have to. His mind reached out, searching.

Their observer wasn't there in person. That always made it harder. A lesser saireishi would have been stuck, but not Madrigan. He found the camera through which they were being watched, and followed it. Like other saireishi, he couldn't reach computers or robots or anything manufactured; that wasn't how his power worked. But a person was aware of the device they used: where it was placed on their side, where it was on the other end, whether it was live, and so on. Madrigan didn't need much detail. So long as a person was vaguely aware — and most people were — that was enough for him to track them down.

He found their observer many decks down, in a small room. The overweight Chaukee gobbled down snacks as he watched the feed, mostly paying attention to Geffin. A second console ran a recognition program.

That was bad. Everyone in the group, save for Madrigan, had a record. The computer would take seconds at most to finish its recognition program and then find the records.

Since there was nothing Madrigan could do about the computer, he focused his attention on the Chaukee. The Chaukee was part of the tech side of the station's security. Watching the monitors comprised his entire job. Most people who had jobs like that found them boring. Since most of the work was done by computers and robots, a sentient being just needed to be there to monitor it all.

Madrigan sank into the Chaukee's mind and almost

groaned aloud at what he found there. Over the years, he'd discovered any number of perversions while exploring minds. There had been one Parleni who liked to get too close to people to smell them. He was guarded once by a Huckfering who enjoyed nothing more than watching people get tortured. He had also met a Human who fantasized about young children. With that man, Madrigan had found a way to expose his fantasies to the authorities. He had since been taken away to be reconditioned — Madrigan was proud of that. But with most people, he tried to ignore the desires he found in their minds.

The Chaukee security tech loved his job — literally loved it. He wanted nothing more than to obverse people from far away. He played with the various camera feeds, zooming in on certain people and certain parts of their anatomy. Some of the best feeds, he saved to his jewel for later, for private perusal.

At the moment, he was more focused on a Sithfin woman than on Madrigan or his associates. However much he enjoyed his job, the pretty people wouldn't distract him from doing it correctly. He desperately didn't want to lose the job because then he would have to watch people in public, where he would be noticed and perhaps arrested.

While the computer worked, Madrigan tightened the Chaukee's attention on the Sithfin woman to give him more time. Once that was done, he slid lower in the man's mind.

The unconscious, natural processes that the brain performed were the hardest to affect. No matter what the holocins said, most saireishi couldn't kill a person by stopping their heart or their brain. Maybe if they stood close to their victim but even then only the most powerful and skilled saireishi could manage such a feat. Madrigan was that powerful and skilled, but the distance was too great. Anyway, he had no desire to kill the Chaukee.

Once he reached the lowest depths of the Chaukee's mind, he reached for his hearing. When the computer finished its search, it would make an audible beep. The Chaukee didn't need to be hard of hearing for long, just a few seconds at exactly the right time. If he went any longer without hearing, he'd notice since his various feeds came with audio. And, when he found a person he particularly enjoyed watching, he wanted to hear them too.

Madrigan didn't notice where he was walking, trusting his comrades to keep him pointed in the right direction. All his attention centered on the Chaukee and the computer. The moment Geffin's name appeared on the monitor, Madrigan shut down the Chaukee's hearing. When the beep came a moment later, the Chaukee didn't notice.

He was good at his job. Even if he hadn't noticed yet, he would check the security feeds soon. Madrigan couldn't control his mind for long. It was far too tiring and distracting.

Archive it, he told the Chaukee, pressing the command deep into the man's mind.

The Chaukee blinked, a handful of snacks halfway to his mouth, his attention still riveted by the Sithfin woman. She'd stopped to examine some items in the market, bending over to offer him an excellent angle. The Chaukee's hearing had returned, and he wanted to listen to the woman's conversation with the shopkeeper. He could manage the day's archive later, at the end of his shift when he usually did it.

Madrigan hated people with firm routines. They were always harder to move. *Archive it,* he said silently, pushing even harder.

With a shake of his head, the Chaukee shoved the snacks into his mouth. Without looking away from the Sithfin women and without pausing his chewing, he reached for the controls. He'd done this thousands of times before, so didn't need to look as he did it again.

The footage for the last few hours got collected and saved, then archived in case it needed to be examined at a later time. It took four buttons to do all that.

Finished, the Chaukee settled back in his chair for some more ogling.

Feeling vaguely ill, Madrigan surfaced. The halls around him had changed at some point. When, he couldn't say. Before, they had walked through clean, crowded corridors. Now, dirt covered everything, there weren't as many lights, and far fewer people trudged past, none of them willing to give the crew a smile or a hello.

When the next person passed, Madrigan leaned closer to Geffin. "Our identities have been archived," he whispered.

Geffin gave a shallow nod. "Good. Any other trouble?"

"Not at the moment."

"How long before someone checks the archive?"

Madrigan shrugged. "Depends on how long it takes for someone to chase us here. Two standard days, at most."

Someone would follow them from Hreckin. The dead bodies and the stolen treasure must have been discovered by now. That sort of crime couldn't be handled internally since Hreckin had only recently become a Neutral world. As such, Hreckin would have called someone to come investigate. Probably Neutral police, but perhaps Gray instead or in addition. Madrigan would prefer a Gray operative for his plan, but Neutral would still work.

When the *Otteran* left Hreckin, they registered their destination. Hreckin could use their sensor logs to check the destination. A ship could easily drop out of hyperspace early and change destinations or arrive at its destination for only a few seconds before making a second jump. Hreckin would assume that the *Otteran* had done one of those things. Still, Waljik 6 had been their listed destination, so someone would come here to check.

They gave their registration here as the *Otteran*, which was the same registration they used on Hreckin. While some of the crew weren't listed on the official manifest, Geffin would be. That would be enough to get their pursuers' full attention. One of the first things that a person would do would be to check the station's security archives. They would then confirm Geffin's presence.

Their pursuer would see Madrigan too, but that didn't matter. He wasn't registered as a saireishi and he didn't have a criminal record. As far as most of the galaxy knew, he was a boring Neutral who'd gone on his first criminal venture. They wouldn't pay much attention to him, not even when they found his jewel. He'd left his extra on the shuttle, and only an incompetent police officer would fail to find it.

He only hoped they wouldn't have to wait for long. If they had to stay here for more than a day, their backups would start to fall apart. That was why Madrigan hoped for a Gray pursuer; they were far better trained than Neutral ones. They had more influence during their pursuits as well, since no one wanted to get on the bad side of the Gray.

When he thought about it, Madrigan felt bad about what would happen to the officers who found him here. They were a necessary loss. They wouldn't die or be injured; he and the rest of the crew couldn't afford that. Likely, this would be a blow to their career, having dangerous criminals in their grasp only to lose them.

Madrigan and Geffin weren't common thieves or murderers. They were on a quest, a plot that would make the galaxy a better place. He hoped that, someday, the rest of the galaxy would understand. Perhaps the rest of the galaxy would even forgive him and the others. So long as the galaxy hated Hreckin and all the people there, that was all that mattered.

If he had to, Madrigan would kill any number of people to ensure that happened. Hreckin would fall. He would guarantee it.

4

The *Nebula's Edge* drifted through space, deep in the Hreckin system. The display had been blank for five minutes. Vilstair glared at the com controls, silently willing them to do something. No matter how much she wished it, no one called her from Hreckin.

"Come on," she said when ten minutes had passed. "How long does it take to track one pirate ship?" Hreckin was a newer planet, without all the latest tech and toys, but surely the government could at least afford basic hyperspace tracking devices. If not, every thief in the galaxy would be hitting this place.

When fifteen minutes passed, her patience, such as it was, ran out. She pushed the com button, opening a channel to the authorities on Hreckin.

An image took over the blankness of her display: a male Chaukee, his dark fur neatly groomed. "What's the problem, Officer Bila?"

She pressed her wide lips together, wishing she had teeth to grind. "You contacted my superiors over an hour ago, sir. I've been here fifteen standard minutes. The thieves are long gone. If I'm to have any chance of finding them, I need to start now."

"We are aware of that, Officer Bila. We're working as fast as we can." His voice was perfectly bland.

Vilstair decided she hated him. "Are your systems

malfunctioning?"

"Everything is working fine. Please maintain your current position. We'll call you when we have an update." The screen turned blank as he hung up.

"Why that stupid little fuc—" Vilstair clapped her lips down on the rest of it. She was an operative. She wasn't supposed to swear. At least not in public.

Which didn't mean she couldn't enjoy a fantasy about the Gray gods slowly killing the man. Vilstair took a moment to do just that.

Calmer now, she opened the com line to HQ on Diresi. Yafan answered immediately, even though it was late at night on Diresi. His lips drooped over his sharp teeth, and his ears tilted down. "What is it now?"

"No one on Hreckin will tell me anything." That sounded whiny. Vilstair scowled. "Do they want the thieves to get away?"

"Who the fuck knows?" Yafan shook himself, a few bits of fur coming off to stick to his neat uniform. "Sorry, Vilstair. We've been inundated. I'll see if I can manage anything. We might have to send a different operative."

Vilstair clamped her mouth shut to keep her jaw from falling open. "Someone else? What for? No one else is nearby! And my record is excellent!" At least the whine was gone from her voice, replaced by fury.

"It isn't your fault. I wish there was someone closer to you. You can't change how people think, no matter how stupid. It's not your fault, Vilstair, and this won't stain your record, I promise." Before Vilstair could ask what he meant, Yafan hung up.

Was something wrong with Hreckin? Besides questionable tech and morons in charge?

She tapped the jewel at her temple. At her mental command, information on Hreckin came up. Since she was inside her ship, the information appeared on the display. Before Vilstair could do more than peruse the list of topics, another call came from the planet.

"You found them?" she asked, answering.

It was a Flimlit on the other end this time, the gills expanding and retracting as he breathed. "Gray Officer Bila? We think we've found a clue, but we need an expert opinion. Can you come down to help?"

"Of course!"

The coordinates for a landing site appeared on the display, after pushing aside the information on Hreckin. It was close to one of the government buildings in the capital. Vilstair grabbed the controls and flew towards the indicated coordinates.

When she approached the atmosphere, it occurred to her that, if she had to stop and consult first, the thieves would get even further away before she could pursue them. Well, she couldn't follow them without information anyway. She would have to hope that the thieves were too stupid to make multiple jumps through hyperspace. If they deviated from the usual routes or made odd stops, the *Nebula's Edge*'s computer wasn't equipped to track them.

Clouds parted, and a large city spread out over a savanna. Strange that she could see wildlife. Most cities had the odd park and not much else. Hreckin was a new world. The inhabitants must not have had time to clear out all the annoying shrubbery yet, and the associated animals.

The buildings hunched near the ground, the tallest barely forty stories. Vilstair wondered why anyone would want to live here, so far from everything else. It was pretty, she supposed. Most worlds with breathable atmospheres had blue skies. Hreckin had an orange sky, giving everything an odd tinge.

Lots of nature lovers must live here, Vilstair decided.

The parking garage rose a block from the center of the capital, with wide openings along the top levels so that ships could easily enter. Vilstair picked a spot on the east side, where the roof was lower. Her ship was a cruiser, so she didn't need much room.

No one was waiting for her.

Frowning, Vilstair loosened her restraints and switched the ship's engine to idle. She didn't shut it down — she might need to leave in a hurry. The skin on the back of her neck turned damp, as it always did when she felt nervous.

Having no one to meet her shouldn't be enough to trigger her instincts. Something else was wrong.

Before leaving the ship, she made sure that her blaster was secure in the holster at her hip. It was turned to stun, as it usually was. Vilstair briefly toyed with the thought of changing the setting, but her training and her experience changed her mind. Whatever was going on here wouldn't be improved if she threatened to kill someone.

She'd been through plenty of dangerous situations before, and she had never yet killed another person. She didn't plan to change that now.

The parking garage was empty, with only a few ships on the far side. Vilstair's steps echoed on the concrete floor. She kept a grip on her blaster as she walked to the stairs. First rule of dangerous situations: never take the lift. Garbage lay strewn in the corners of each landing, and Vilstair wished her nose wasn't so good. Most species wouldn't be bothered by the smell, but she was.

By the time she reached the ground floor, she still hadn't seen anyone. Was it a holiday on Hreckin? To her relief, when she left the parking garage, she saw people wandering the sidewalks. Small, inner-atmospheric ships flew low to the ground, skimming the heads of the people passing underneath.

Though she waited a few moments while looking around, she still didn't see anyone here to meet her.

The government building was down the block. If they wouldn't come to her, she'd go to them. Vilstair started down the sidewalk.

In her years as a Gray operative, she'd visited many worlds. All of them were Gray or Neutral, established and registered for centuries. This was the first newly registered world she'd ever visited. She had known to expect a few strange things, but she didn't anticipate the way everyone stared at her.

The people on the street stopped to gape at her. Ships overhead slowed down and turned so that people could stare through the windows. One human woman made a rude gesture, then flew so low that Vilstair had to duck.

"What in the hells is wrong with this place?" She picked up her pace. She wanted to be out of here as soon as possible.

When she reached the door of the government building, she received her answer. "Ill-gotten," one of the guards said when he saw her.

Vilstair froze, one foot a few inches in the air. "Excuse me?"

"You're Ill-gotten, aren't you? You have to be. No natural person looks that ugly."

Her hand clenched around her blaster. If there hadn't been so many people about, she might have shot the guard. "I am Gray Officer Vilstair Bila, on assignment to assist your government with the apprehension of the thieves who broke into the treasury. I was called over to help with the investigation." Years of professionalism kept her voice calm, but it was a struggle.

The guard shook his head, his antenna waving with the motion. "That can't be right. We would never ask someone like you for help." The people nearby had stopped to watch,

51

murmuring softly to one another. Even the robots who helped guard stared at her, their lights flickering in a regular pattern.

When she spoke to him, Yafan said something about how the people of Hreckin thought — and that whatever happened here wouldn't be held against her. Apart from the Light and a few, painfully primitive worlds, she'd never heard of anyone prejudiced against Ill-gotten — at least, not openly.

That Flimlit who called: who had he been? Had she checked his credentials? Had she even checked the location from where he called? A prank call? Or, worse, a call to set her up for this humiliation?

Since she was unique in the galaxy, at least she didn't show her embarrassment in ways that other people could spot. No one who wasn't her friend could guess her body language, and no one here would ever be her friend. Moisture hung between her fingers, but not enough to start dripping. The idiots here would probably mistake that for an attack.

Even if the call from the Flimlit had been a sham, the Gray police had still sent her out here to assist. She was on the planet already. Maybe if she made a nuisance of herself, she could finally get some information.

"I am here on behalf of the Gray, sir. Do you intend to deny me?"

He opened his beak, but nothing came out. "No," he said after a few more attempts.

The Gray was the most powerful force in the galaxy. Vilstair gave thanks for that often and fervently. "Then you will lead me to the Treasury so that I may offer assistance."

"Fine." He shifted his shoulders and glared at the other guards, who wore too-wide smirks. "It's down the street, ma'am." With steps that were too rigid and with his neck-feathers sticking out, the guard led her away from the one building, towards another. Vilstair spotted the sign, her jewel making it larger. She should have started at the Treasury. That way, she could have avoided some of this annoyance.

Though she received plenty more looks during the short walk, she pretended to be oblivious. At least no one shouted with the guard nearby. She waited a few paces away to be polite while the first guard talked with those outside the Treasury, explaining her presence. Vilstair tried not to hear, but it was hard to miss the first guard saying, "She's Ill-gotten, so she has no manners. If we don't let her in, she might attack us!"

She had to force her hand away from her blaster. Did he think she was a rabid animal? Fine, her parents were different species, and she'd been conceived and grown in a laboratory. She was raised the same as everyone else. No, she'd been raised better — unlike these assholes, she had manners.

When the first guard came to fetch her, a Human guard accompanied him. Vilstair briefly thought a Human might be better. Like most Ill-gottens, Vilstair was half-Human. Human genes mixed better with alien genes. The resulting children had a much higher rate of survival. The look on the face of the Human guard told her in advance that her hopes would not be enough.

"Only officials from Hreckin are allowed on a crime scene, Officer," the Human guard said, his freckles bright in the sunlight.

"Your superiors requested assistance from the Gray. As a newly registered Neutral world, perhaps you do not appreciate what that means. You're involved in politics now, sir, and I can't leave until my mission is complete. Or perhaps you'd like to explain things to the Gray high command?"

His fair skin turned paler, and Vilstair repressed a smile. That would teach him to mess with the Gray. No one wanted the attention of the Gray high command. "You will not touch anything at the scene." Without waiting for a response, he pivoted and marched into the building. Vilstair followed him. Her earlier guide stayed behind, presumably to head back to his post.

Everyone inside the Treasury looked official, dressed in colorful suits and with their jewels displaying identification. They all stopped and stared at Vilstair, as much for her uniform as for anything else. Assholes they might be, but at least they knew how to respect a Gray officer.

A few hours ago, the thieves broke into the vault under the Treasury, taking physical currency, old coins and jewels, and a number of objects of historical significance. When Yafan sent Vilstair here, he gave her a list of everything the thieves took. She skimmed the list earlier, on her flight to Hreckin.

The remnants of the vault door hung to the side, barely clinging on. Scorch marks littered it, the walls outside, and the inside of the vault. The thieves hadn't been quiet. It was early morning when they struck, and people had been here. Though the bodies had already been taken away, Vilstair saw the outlines on the ground of where those bodies fell. Four of them.

Never mind that she hated everyone on Hreckin. She would find these thieves and bring them to justice. They were murderers now, which no one thought to tell her before.

"Why didn't you mention this?" she asked, waving at the outlines. "Or did you not think the Gray needed to know?" The question was addressed to her escort and to everyone else within hearing distance. When worlds contracted with the Gray, they were expected to provide all the necessary information. A world that asked for help but refused to offer intelligence would soon be refused aid by the Gray.

An older Nwist stepped out of the vault. He wore an expensive suit that strained over the two segments of his torso. Bands of gold glittered at his neck, his four wrists, and his four ankles. He loomed high over Vilstair and looked down a prominent nose at her. "You are Officer Bila?"

"Yes, sir."

"You are liaising with us to find and apprehend the thieves. You will bring them in alive so that they can stand trial. In case I was not clear, they will stand trial here, not Diresi. Their crimes were against Hreckin, not the Gray."

Vilstair's skin grew moister at the nape of her neck, a reaction she couldn't help. His tone angered her more than anything else. "So, you thought I didn't need to know? People who are willing to kill once are willing to kill a second time. That's something I need to know as I track them down. Assuming anyone ever tells me where to look." Though she had to crane her head back to look him in the eye, Vilstair didn't lose eye contact. Neither did she blink. Thanks to her mixed genes, she always won staring contests.

"If you were in such a hurry to apprehend the thieves, you would have stayed in your ship in orbit."

"I was asked to come down here."

The Nwist narrowed his eyes. "By whom?"

She didn't know who, and she probably shouldn't have come down. She wasn't about to admit that. "The call came from this building, sir. Whatever your feelings about me personally, you cannot ignore me. Not unless you wish to offend the entire Gray. Do you know where the thieves are? Or at least their trajectory?"

The Nwist glanced to his side. A female Parleni appeared, a jewel on both bald temples. "Here are the coordinates, sir." She tapped the jewel on her right temple. Her thick lips curled into a sneer as she stared at Vilstair. She of all people shouldn't judge Vilstair's appearance — Vilstair was half-Parleni.

Vilstair pressed her jewel in turn, receiving the information. The thieves' trajectory had Waljik 6, a Neutral station in deep space. As a Gray operative, Vilstair could visit any Neutral world or station without waiting for permission. She had to register her presence and mission with the local government, but they would allow her to work without oversight or interference. She hadn't needed permission to land on Hreckin — she'd only stayed so long in her ship so she could start her pursuit sooner.

"Thank you. As soon as you uncover additional information, you will pass it on to me. Likewise, I will keep you updated on my hunt." That was standard practice, but these people clearly knew nothing and thus needed the reminder.

With a quick salute, Vilstair turned to head out of the building.

"Wait, Officer," the official said.

She had made it two whole steps. Seething silently, she pivoted to face him again. "The longer I wait, the further away the thieves will get, sir."

"They will not have gone far. They want you to catch up with them."

Vilstair twitched. "What? How do you—"

The Nwist ignored her, looking at the Parleni again. "Is Kyran Jorn available?"

"Yes, sir. He's in the capital."

"Excellent. Have him meet us outside." The official strode past Vilstair towards the lift. His four legs ate up the distance with a regular clatter, and Vilstair had to jog to keep up with him. The three of them, along with four guards, rode the elevator up. The Parleni turned her head to make the call.

Vilstair took a few deep breaths before speaking. "Sir, having a local accompany me is not standard practice. As you saw, these thieves are willing to kill to get what they want. I cannot guarantee the safety of Kyran Jorn if he comes with me."

"No need, Officer. Being Jorn has a very capable

bodyguard. Anyway, he'll be chasing down the thieves regardless of what you want, so you might as well travel together."

That sounded like something with a lot of history. Vilstair tried again. "My ship is registered to the Gray. Only military personnel, operatives, military-adjacent persons, and persons of interest to a case are allowed on board." She could bend those rules if she wanted to — Order was preferred, but knew how to adjust when the situation demanded it. At the moment, she didn't want to bend the rules. She was counting on them, actually.

"Being Jorn has a deep interest in this case, Officer, so it's not a problem. Here we are." The lift doors beeped as they opened, and the official stepped out first, one of the guards hurrying to keep pace with him.

Vilstair wished she had a smaller ship because then she'd have an additional excuse. As it was, her ship would fit two additional people.

They stopped in a large foyer before the main doors to the building. Columns lined the circumference of the foyer, with fruit sculpted along the tops and bottoms. Every little noise echoed off the marble floors, but at least there weren't many people about, most instead lingering at the sides and hallways that lead off the foyer.

Vilstair had no idea who Kyran Jorn was. When she spotted a group of reporters mobbing in one place, her stomach sank. Oh hells, no. Not a celebrity. She'd put up with constant insults to her genetics rather than a celebrity.

A year ago, she had to interview a celebrity for information on a case. That had been bad enough. She couldn't imagine having to work in close quarters with one.

"There he is," the official said with a smile. He looked right at the reporters because sometimes the gods hated Vilstair. At his approach, the reporters stepped back but didn't move away. Vilstair saw what had commanded their attention, and her heart skipped a beat.

She knew that man. In holocins, he went by Koryanran Joranran, and he was one of the biggest stars in the galaxy. He'd been in so many holocins — Vilstair's brain helpfully supplied a list of the best ones, along with how many times she drooled over his performances. Even bad holocins were elevated when he was in them. Many people agreed that he was the best actor alive, a sentiment with which Vilstair heartily agreed.

His dark hair fell messy and perfect across his brow as he turned to see them, his blue eyes electric. He gave the official a smile so white it would blind a Light path. Vilstair wished he'd look at her that way. "Councilor Grisher! Excellent. Any news on the thieves?"

"We know their trajectory. Officer Bila is from the Gray to help us find them and bring them to justice." The Nwist gestured towards Vilstair.

Joranran turned his attention to her, and Vilstair's knees went weak. He was actually looking at her — at her! "H-Hello." How the word ever made it out of her mouth, she didn't know.

"Thank you for letting me accompany you, Officer. I want to be able to reclaim my property as soon as possible. And my bodyguard will be very helpful, I'm sure." He inclined his head towards a bulky Drilthin who hovered beside him.

Vilstair barely noticed as that would involve looking away from Joranran. "Of course. Whatever you want."

"Wonderful!" His smile dipped an inch. That was enough to make Vilstair worry. Anything that kept his smile from being perfect was something that should be fixed — or permanently removed. Joranran cleared his throat and leaned closer, voice pitched low. "Will, ah, will we be able to manage on our own?"

"Of course we will. Why wouldn't we?"

Joranran glanced at the Nwist and shrugged. "Well, I'm sure the Gray trains all its operatives, and I would never think to say anything against the Gray. It's just… Well, will you be able to overcome the difficulties?"

"What difficulties? So long as we have coordinates, we can track the thieves through hyperspace." If the thieves left the normal routes, they might have trouble, but Vilstair could always contact the Gray for assistance and equipment.

"No, I meant with—" Joranran slid nearer still, and Vilstair knew she'd never been happier in her whole life. Though he spoke quietly, it was loud enough for the reporters to pick up the conversation. "Will you have problems? With your genetic limitations, I mean?"

Vilstair's mouth opened and answered without input from her brain. "I'm just a stupid Ill-gotten, but I'm sure with your help, the thieves will be found."

"How wonderful!" Joranran turned his smile back to max for the cameras.

When he turned away, sense returned to Vilstair. Her stomach turned, and she had to clench her jaw shut to keep it closed. What in the hells had just happened? She would never, never say anything like that! It didn't matter who asked, she would never mock herself! She worked too hard to get respect to do that.

Heat filled her, and she wished she could disappear. In one moment of celebrity-induced stupidity, she'd completely undercut herself, other Ill-gottens, and the Gray.

After that level of stupidity, she didn't deserve to be working this case.

I can't do anything for Madrigan. I've tried — the gods know how I've tried. Maybe one day I can do something. Yonaven says so. That's one of the reasons she uses to get me to focus on other people. When Madrigan's asleep, sometimes I obey Yonaven and practice on other people. I'd like to practice on Yonaven, but I can't.

"You have so few limits," Yonaven says, "but you have to practice. Even things that come naturally have to be practiced. Babies aren't born walking or even crawling."

"I wouldn't know about walking or crawling." That makes her feel guilty. I can tell. There's nothing I love better than making Yonaven feel bad. Yeah, it's petty. If you were trapped in my life, you'd enjoy the petty stuff too.

The things I try on other people, the things I'd like to try on Yonaven — I don't try those things on Madrigan. I only want good things for him. Maybe there's a way to be kind, but I don't know it yet. I haven't practiced enough for gentleness.

When Madrigan met Geffin, I almost tried something. Not on Madrigan, but on Geffin. I didn't, and it turned out to be a good thing. I didn't need to do anything to make them friends.

Friendship is a beautiful thing. I don't know much about it. I don't have any friends. But Madrigan has friends, and I know everything about Madrigan. It's a weird thing, friendship. At first, I was willing to do mean things to Geffin. Then I put up with him. Now I like him almost as much as Madrigan.

Sometimes, when Madrigan is asleep and when Yonaven isn't pestering me, I dream. My eyes are already closed, and my mind is already far away, but I wasn't dreaming before. I slip away, farther than even I can reach, and I see the future.

The future I see in my dreams is amazing. Madrigan is there, with Geffin and the rest of his friends. They're happy and rich and helping to make the galaxy better for Ill-gottens. They've got a purpose, something more than money, and they love it. It isn't a perfect future — I can't imagine that much happiness — but it's beautiful.

When I'm asleep a long time and the dream goes far enough, then I appear. Madrigan hears about me and comes for me. He saves me a second time, lifting me up and carrying me away from here.

I don't like that dream. That's one of the reasons I don't like to sleep for very long. Whenever I see that dream, I wake up. I hate waking up. Waking up makes me notice my life. Of all the cruel things that have been done to me, that is the worst. Because I am alone and because Madrigan doesn't know about me and because even he couldn't rescue me.

No one can save me. Fate has decreed that I will be here for the rest of my life.

5

"I need to check your ship."

The deep voice, sudden and close, shook Vilstair from her despair. When she noticed how close the Drilthin stood to her, she almost jumped. She forced the reaction down. She'd been unprofessional enough to last a year. She needed to get her head on straight, and now.

"Is there a problem with my ship?" The Drilthin was Joranran's bodyguard. "I'm sorry, I didn't catch your name?"

"Butler." Large, beady eyes stared down at her from either side of the horn that protruded from his nose, as if daring her to contradict that name. Drilthins were the most popular bodyguards in the galaxy, their powerful frames sufficient to intimidate almost anyone. During her academy days, Vilstair trained with a Drilthin. Kebet was one of the sweetest, funniest people she knew, who went into logistics because she couldn't handle the idea of harming another being. Naturally, Kebet was a Lifer, but that never was a problem for the two of them.

Vilstair rocked back on her heels so that she could look Butler in the eyes but not step back. "I understand that you're paid to be concerned for Being Joranran's well-fare, but I assure you that my ship is safe. It has the best Gray security on it."

His large nostril's flared. "I will still need to inspect it before Being Jorn boards."

"You can go inside first if you want. I'm in a parking garage a block away." She waved in the general direction.

"Being Jorn doesn't walk around like an ordinary person. We will bring the ship here."

"It'll be faster if we all go together. The thieves are already hours ahead of us."

Butler shook his head, his stiff mane only twitching a little. "It will be faster if we bring your ship here."

If Joranran walked along the street, a mob of people would form around them. Maybe Butler had a point. Vilstair nodded, and together with a guard, they left the Treasury building. Though she didn't need a guide, the guard accompanied her to the parking garage and then up to the correct floor. At least he stopped outside the lift instead of following all the way to her ship.

Vilstair pressed one hand flat to the panel next to the door, the other pressing the jewel at her temple. A soft beep came as the *Nebula's Edge* recognized her, and the door opened down into a ramp. Butler entered first, tapping his jewel as he looked around. He checked everything, even the hold and the decontamination shower.

Finally, Butler waved for Vilstair to move the ship. She huffed, pushing down her annoyance. This was her ship: only she decided when to leave.

It took less than a minute to reach the lawn outside the Treasury Building, which was just large enough to fit the *Nebula's Edge*. Butler opened the door and gestured. Joranran walked from the building and inside the ship.

"Sorry about the mess," Vilstair said, suddenly spotting the remains of dinner on the small table. She grabbed the plate and dumped its contents into the incinerator, only to realize a moment later that she'd also just thrown out the fork. That was fine. She had extra forks. She stuffed the plate into the washer and fixed a smile on her face.

"It's quaint." Joranran smiled as he turned slowly in the center of the ship.

Quaint. Vilstair pressed her lips together. The *Nebula's Edge* was a cruiser-class ship, standard for a Gray operative. It had three beds which folded out from the wall, a wide hold, a comfortable couch opposite the beds, a refresher and a decontamination shower, plus enough armaments to take out most other ship of the same class. Like most Gray operatives, Vilstair spent as much time in the ship as she did planet-side. More so even than her apartment on Diresi, the *Nebula's Edge* was home.

Joranran must have noticed her expression because his smile softened. "I'm sorry. I know this is the best the Gray can offer someone like you. It's lovely, and thank you for letting us accompany you."

Vilstair moved through the common area of the ship to the cockpit. When she was seated in the pilot's chair, she felt secure. Whatever else, this was her ship. And it had all sorts of fun things that Joranran didn't know about.

A tap of her jewel fed the coordinates into the ship's nav computer. "Please sit down," she said, fastening her restraints.

Though he hadn't been invited, Joranran took the co-pilot's seat, his blue eyes dancing as he looked at the display. Vilstair decided that this was the best place for him. Butler loomed in the door to the cockpit, using strong arms to brace himself against the sides. If he wanted to stay like that as they passed through the atmosphere, that was his choice.

Vilstair revved the engine, glad she'd left it loitering. The *Nebula's Edge* maneuvered slowly off the lawn of the Treasury Building, then picked up speed and turned vertical once they made it past the highest buildings. The ship's artificial gravity meant that Butler didn't have to strain to stay in place. As the ship accelerated upwards, Vilstair felt a little pressure.

Joranran must have felt it too because he gasped. "I can feel us moving!"

"This is a small ship, sir. It can't cut off all of gravity's effects."

"Don't apologize!" Joranran said, even though no one had. "It's awesome!"

The ship broke away from the planet's gravity, the pressure dying away. If Vilstair had flown slower, they would have felt nothing. The thieves had hours ahead of them, and they'd wasted enough time.

She continued further away from the planet until a com came from the planet to confirm she could safely jump to hyperspace. Jumping close to a planet wouldn't hurt the planet, but it could ruin a ship. And being crushed while jumping was a nasty way to die.

Since the coordinates were already in the nav computer, Vilstair yanked the jump lever. The stars streaked into lines as the *Nebula's Edge* passed into hyperspace.

If the thieves had indeed stopped at Waljik 6, it would take an hour to reach them. Vilstair swiveled to Joranran. "You have a connection to the thieves? What is it?"

He rubbed the back of his neck. The way he held his head made him look boyish and lovely. Vilstair's stomach did something funny again. "Ah, well, I've been a sponsor of the Hreckin government for years. They're only recently Neutral, so they need help. They're a new planet, but I believe in what they stand for. Anyway, I've given them lots of money, but other things too. The thieves took one of those things."

What the hells did that mean, what Hreckin stood for? It was another new colony, no different from the thousands of other colonies that constantly sprang up. The galaxy was huge: they hadn't explored half of it yet. Exploration and scientific ships checked one system after another, looking for new life and planets that could sustain life. Or planets with useful resources.

One such ship found Hreckin one hundred fifty standard years ago. Once it was determined that no sentient life already claimed the planet, the explorers set safe hyperspace routes to Hreckin, and the pilgrims began to arrive. People settled new planets for any number of reasons: hoping to get rich, hoping to build a new life, looking to make discoveries, trying to escape law enforcement, or being forced into an alignment. As a good Gray, Vilstair didn't judge those people — well, except those escaping the law. The Light decried people who tried to avoid committing to an alignment, but the Gray did not. Their path was superior to all the others, of course, but a person was free to pick whatever they liked best. Some people were more comfortable with the Light or Neutral. There were even people who went Dark, but Vilstair tried not to think about those people. Thank all the Gray gods, her work never took her close to Dark space.

"If you gave it to Hreckin, it's theirs now," she said instead of the question she wanted to ask. She should have done more research on Hreckin on her flight here.

Joranran clicked his tongue. "You don't understand. It isn't your fault."

Right. She could ignore lots of things, but not that. Not here on her ship, with nothing else to distract her. She crossed her arms over her chest and scowled at him. From the doorway, Butler made a soft, dangerous whuff, but Vilstair ignored him. He couldn't hurt her in her own ship. Not with the security measures the *Nebula's Edge* had.

"What do you and everyone else on Hreckin have against Ill-gotten? And don't say there isn't anything."

His blue eyes looked sad suddenly. "I don't blame you, Officer. Nor do I blame any other Ill-gotten. You had no choice in how you were conceived. It's just… Well, you aren't natural. If the gods intended for people like you to exist, you wouldn't have needed a test tube."

"It wasn't a test tube." Most people knew little about how Ill-gotten children were conceived or grown. She had no intention of going into technical details, mostly because she suspected that wouldn't help. "If the gods didn't want me here, I wouldn't be here. And I know the gods better than you do." She gave him a pointed look.

"You know the Gray gods better than me. Do you even know the names of the others?"

His eyes were getting increasingly less pretty. Maybe the lighting in her ship didn't suit him. "I know about all the gods. I don't just deal with Gray paths." Thus far, she hadn't had to deal with Dark paths, and she hoped that would continue. She hadn't dealt with the Light either, which, though less terrifying, was equally nice to avoid.

Joranran leaned back in his chair. "The gods take a less personal hand in things these days. They leave most business to the lords. If the gods still paid attention, you wouldn't be here."

"Order loves me." No matter what else, Vilstair never doubted that. Like most operatives in law enforcement, she was a dedicated follower of Order. The entire galaxy should love Order: then, there would be no crime or rebellion. Everyone would know their place and be content with it.

"An Orderer? I guess that makes sense with your profession, but not with anything else. Well, you seem better than most Ill-gotten. You must be exceptional, to become a Gray operative."

Vilstair rubbed her lips together, trying to compose herself. On the one hand, she had worked long and hard to reach her current position, and she was proud of what she'd done. She liked being called exceptional. On the other hand, she thought she had reached this point in part because of who she was, not in spite of it.

Many Ill-gotten combinations weren't viable. Those that were tended to manage better than normal people. People like Vilstair had been engineered from the beginning. Any deformations or undesirable traits had been taken away before she had been born.

She stared at the star lines outside. Maybe she wasn't as good as she'd thought. After all, she admitted in front of cameras that she was a stupid Ill-gotten.

How that had escaped her mouth, she still didn't know. She didn't think that. She'd never thought that.

"The thieves are at the Waljik 6 station," Butler said. He lingered in the doorway to the cockpit, now leaning against the side of the door. He didn't look at Vilstair the way Joranran did, as if she were a child in need of help. Instead, he watched her as if worried she might attack Joranran. Neither option pleased Vilstair, and she prayed that this mission would end quickly and successfully. "That isn't a safe place."

Ten stations drifted through deep space in this region of the galaxy, at the edge of new space. All the Waljik stations were rough places, stopping off points for people heading deeper into the unknown or to the recently discovered. They were Neutral, but only officially. Vilstair didn't have to check records to know that those stations were popular among smugglers and thieves and pirates and other undesirables. It was an obvious place for their quarry to head, which was why she hoped they hadn't veered off elsewhere.

"You should stay inside the *Nebula's Edge*, Being Joranran." They had fifteen minutes yet before they arrived.

He huffed. "Please don't joke. I'm here to help retrieve what was taken. I can't do that if I stay behind like a coward. I'm going."

Vilstair glanced at Butler. He didn't look happy with the way his large nostrils flared, and he thrust at the air with his horn, but he didn't argue. He must be used to Joranran.

She tapped her jewel to bring up all the information she had gotten from Hreckin. The coordinates for Waljik 6 popped onto the display, as was a repeat of the list of stolen items. That was it. Frowning, she tapped her jewel again, but no additional information appeared. "They have to know more than that."

"What else do we need to know?" Joranran said.

"Oh, I don't know, the registration of their ship?" That had come out darker than she'd intended. Vilstair rubbed her lips together again, but didn't apologize for her tone.

If the thieves had left Waljik 6, they needed that registration to continue the chase. Even if they were still there on Waljik 6, the station was a big place with plenty of ships. Vilstair needed to know which one she wanted. A list of the crew would also help in case she needed to chase them down inside the station.

Joranran considered. "Yes, I can see how that might help. Here you go." He tapped his jewel.

Additional information appeared on the display: everything Vilstair wanted and more. Each thief was named and pictured, with DNA patterns for most of them, since they had criminal records. The specs of their ship, the *Otteran*, also appeared. It was a frigate, with more weapons than Vilstair liked and a good ten times the size of the *Nebula's Edge*. She couldn't take them in a space battle.

"What in the hells are these people doing free?" Most of the thieves had prior convictions and had done time in various Neutral jails. Four of them should still be in prison.

"They're a scary bunch, aren't they? Don't worry. Butler can take them. He can defeat anyone."

Vilstair ignored Joranran, something she wouldn't have been able to do a few minutes ago. He no longer held the appeal he once did.

In hyperspace, she couldn't communicate with anyone or

download new information. Her computer held plenty of information that she needed to do your job, which included files on convicts.

Twelve days ago, there had been an escape from the Neutral prison on Fronzesh. She had heard about it at the time, but hadn't paid it much attention. Escapes from Neutral prisons were common, at least when compared with other prisons. Four of the Hreckin thieves had been among those who escaped Fronzesh.

Various outsiders had helped with the escape. Listed most prominently among the names was Geffin Chardan.

"Fucking useless Neutral prisons." This was the eighth breakout to occur from that jail in the last standard year. What was the point of a prison that couldn't hold its occupants?

"Officer! You shouldn't speak like that!"

From anyone else, she might have accepted the scolding. At any other time, she would have been ashamed to use such language aloud. Right now and with Joranran, she didn't care.

"The leader of our thieves has now been involved in breakouts from Fronzesh three times. Why do you keep sending him there?" This deep into unmapped space, there weren't that many other prisons around. On the other hand, it didn't take that much longer to transport convicts to secure prisons. There was a Gray prison only three hours' flight from Hreckin.

"I'm sure there's a reason, just as I'm sure I couldn't comment on matters of security," Joranran said primly. "Whatever the reason, it doesn't matter right now. He escaped, his friends escaped, and we need to catch him. As he's a famous man in these parts — or should I say infamous? — he should be easy to find."

Vilstair's head ached. A famous criminal. Exactly what

she didn't need.

Since Geffin Chardan was famous, at least the computer on her ship contained some information on him. She pressed her lips together as she considered the list of his crimes — a substantial list, certainly, but not as bad as some of the criminals Vilstair had chased. An expert thief who liked to hit government or commercial targets, rather than private collectors. That meant he thought himself a man of principals — or one who liked a challenge.

Until now, none of his priors had involved murder. What had changed? Perhaps not everyone in his new gang got along.

For the rest of the trip through hyperspace, Vilstair studied files on the gang members, as well as the layout of Waljik 6. She wasn't as prepared as she would like, but at least she had something. It was more than she had when she arrived at Hreckin.

A few seconds before exiting hyperspace, she raised the ship's shields. While she didn't expect to be attacked, it was better to be safe. Gray policy held that one should always have shields raised when leaving hyperspace, even when said exit wasn't in Gray territory.

She pressed a button, and the star lines braked to a stop in single points. The closest sun hung distant, a gas giant in between. The Waljik 6 station drifted through space, a long cylinder turning slowly on its side, stabilizing fins and docking bays sticking out.

Numerous ships orbited the station, with smaller crafts docked at its many hangars. The registrations for those ships appeared on the *Nebula's Edge*'s display — another Gray standard practice was to have sensors on when leaving hyperspace. Though the words and pictures zipped past too fast for Vilstair to absorb any details, she saw that most of the ships were Neutral.

With a beep, one registration dominated the display. The *Otteran* was still here. Vilstair let out a breath she didn't remember holding. That was one thing gone right.

The *Otteran* was a frigate-class, too large to dock at the station. It flew closer than most of the ships, making no strange or threatening motions. The *Otteran*'s shields were up, but that was true of most of the ships in the area.

"Hello, Waljik 6. This is Koryanran Joranran on the Gray ship *Nebula's Edge*, requesting permission to dock." Without asking for permission, Joranran opened a com channel to the station.

When Vilstair leaned over to smack his hand away from the controls, Butler made a growling sound. She glanced over her shoulder to see him grasping the hilt of his blaster.

"This is my ship!" she hissed, glaring.

"Yes, but I know the thieves and the area." Joranran smiled as permission came over the com. "Thank you," he said, leaning closer to the controls. "Can you help us? We're looking for a Human called Geffin Chardan, from the *Otteran*."

Vilstair smashed her lips together. "We are here on an official investigation," she said, loud enough for the com to pick it up. "Your assistance is required."

"Understood," said someone on the other end — only audio came through. "The commandant will be waiting for you, Being Joranran." A second confirmation came of which dock to use.

Vilstair gripped the controls tighter than she needed to as she steered the ship closer. The *Nebula's Edge* was small enough to park anywhere, one of the reasons she used it. There were times she needed her ship nearby. "I am the Gray operative here. Please leave the official business to me when we reach the station."

"Of course!" Joranran waved a hand. "I'll let you take

charge until there's trouble."

There were hundreds of things she could say to that. She had to fight to keep them all inside. *I am representing the Gray,* she reminded herself. *I have to be professional no matter what.* She repeated that a few times, but her headache didn't go away. Why did she allow Joranran to come along? Anyone else, even another celebrity, she would have refused.

Stupid crush. She knew better now when it was too late to ditch him.

The *Nebula's Edge* eased into a hangar on the starboard side of the station, amongst many other crafts of the same size and basic shape. Even with their engines off, some of their systems remained on, including the basic com channel, which showed registrations. These were all Neutral ships, most belonging to private citizens.

Vilstair parked her ship in berth 12-GT and powered down most of the systems. As she flipped switches, Joranran stood and left the cockpit, Butler following him. Before she could stand, her jewel pinged as she received a message.

Yafan appeared before her eyes, a private link that didn't show up on the now-darkened display. "You're at Waljik 6 now? Did you get anything else from the Hreckin officials?"

"Not really. I got stuck with Koyranran Joranran."

Yafan twitched his whiskers, his ears drooping. "What, the actor? What in the hells is he doing there?"

"It's a long story." She rubbed her temple, just above where the jewel sat. When she didn't hear anything from further back in the ship, she wondered if Joranran had ditched her. Dread coiling in her gut, she hurried from the cockpit. "He wants to run the investigation. Send me anything that might help."

Yafan said something, which Vilstair missed because Joranran and Butler had already stepped out of the *Nebula's Edge.* Whatever Yafan said, her jewel would record. She could fetch the information later once she didn't have a celebrity to wrangle.

A Human female in a blue suit waited outside the ship, her dark hair pulled back severely, making her face look too wide. "Being Joranran? I'm Vima Thurfond. I will escort you through the station and answer any questions you have."

Before Joranran could speak, Vilstair inserted herself between him and Vima. "Gray Officer Vilstair Bila. This is my investigation."

Vima glanced between Vilstair and Joranran, as if looking to him for confirmation, even though Vilstair had her jewel transmit her credentials. The headache spiked again, and Vilstair had to fight back the grimace.

"It's true," Joranran said, far too cheerful. "I'm just here to look good." He winked at Vima.

The Human's cheeks went pink as she caught her breath. "I'm sure you'll be a great help to the investigation, Being Joranran. It's Geffin Chardan from the *Otteran* you're looking for, right? This way, please. The shuttle from the *Otteran* is in this hangar." She didn't once look at Vilstair through her speech.

Joranran walked beside Vima, flashing his perfect smile down on her. She giggled and touched her hair. Butler ranged around them, glaring at the surroundings.

Unnoticed, Vilstair came last. How in the hells had this happened? More importantly, how did she regain control? Her training had covered many things, but not this.

The com to Yafan was still open. He must have heard the exchange because he said, "Don't worry, Vilstair. We know this isn't your fault. I've sent someone to help, so just hold on."

She pressed her lips together. So, not only did everyone on Hreckin think she needed help, the people back home thought that too. That made this even worse.

"I don't need help. I can manage." Her voice shook as she tried to keep quiet enough that Vima and Joranran couldn't hear.

"You need a partner." Yafan spoke kindly, soothingly. "You're outside of Gray space. You aren't supposed to be alone. I know you just lost Writhim, but you need someone. This has nothing to do with you, Vilstair. It's standard procedure."

Vilstair grimaced. What with dealing with the theft and the chase and then handling Joranran, she'd completely forgotten about Writhim. He'd been her partner, and he was dead. It didn't matter that they'd only worked together a short time or that she'd captured his murderer. It had been less than a day, and already she'd forgotten about him.

His funeral hadn't happened yet. Could she make it back in time? The mission to Hreckin was supposed to have been short and simple.

"Yes, sir. Have them contact me when they arrive at the station. Er, it's someone who won't be distracted by Joranran, right?"

For a moment, only silence came over the com line. Distant noise echoed across the hangar, the metal of the structure amplifying everything. It wasn't enough to mute the string of curses that then came from Yafan.

"You sent a Human female?" Vilstair's voice rose, and she fought it softer. "Yafan! That won't help!"

"I'm sorry! I didn't think about it! Shinead is the closest operative who's not on a mission and without a partner! Don't worry. I'm sure she'll be sensible."

As Vima lead them towards the other end of the hangar, they passed a group of three females from three different species. Joranran paused to smile and wave, which caused all three women to sigh and turn weak at the knees. Observing that, and recalling her own reaction to Joranran, Vilstair knew that Shinead would be no help.

* * *

"There's the shuttle from the *Otteran*." Vima nodded her head towards the craft at the end of the row in the hangar.

The shuttle was a plain affair, with no markings on its bluish exterior. Its height suggested at least two floors of seating, or perhaps one row over a large hold. When Vilstair tapped her jewel, her sensors couldn't penetrate the hold. Her jewel had only basic sensors, so even a little bit of padding would be enough to disguise the interior. A robot listed beside the entry ramp, which stood open. Other than that, it was quiet around the shuttle.

"Where are all the people from the *Otteran*?" Joranran asked as if he had any idea how to conduct an investigation.

Under normal circumstances, Vilstair might have waited for an answer. They needed to find the crew of the *Otteran*, and Vima might know their whereabouts. After hours of frustration, she wanted to do something, and she didn't care what.

With a single, fluid motion, she drew her blaster and flipped off the safety. It was set to stun, as it always was, but the sight of it made her companions stiffen. Butler scowled and reached towards his blaster.

"Stay here," Vilstair told them. "I'm going to check the shuttle." She didn't wait for a response, striding rapidly towards the shuttle. The ramp was open, so she'd have no trouble getting inside.

At her approach, the robot tilted up and spun between her and the ramp. "Identification required for entry," it said.

"I'm a Gray officer, and this is official business." She'd transmitted her credentials to Vima, and she hadn't stopped afterward. The robot received the transmission too. The lights along its front panel flashed in a variety of colors as it processed, probably trying to figure out what to do. The robot belonged to thieves and murderers. Vilstair couldn't assume that normal, robotic protocols would still be running in it.

She shot the robot. The red beam struck its domed head. The lights on its torso all lit up at the same time, then went dead as the robot powered down. It would cycle back up in a few minutes, more than enough time for Vilstair to check the shuttle.

Since they left the robot behind to guard it, the thieves didn't lock the shuttle or even close the door. Vilstair walked right in, blaster held at ready in case anyone lurked inside. She saw no one in the large seating area. Her jewel registered no life signs, but it couldn't penetrate the entire shuttle. Not yet dropping her guard, Vilstair moved deeper. She stuck her head in the cockpit — powered down, so she couldn't access the ship computer, unfortunately — then walked down the stairs at the back to check the large hold. Crates filled half the hold, each neatly labeled.

Vilstair scanned the code on the side of the crates, marking them with her jewel. Wherever these crates went, she would be able to follow. The thieves hadn't thought to avoid using standard marking labels — something, admittedly, most people never thought about.

In the small refresher in the hold, she found a jewel on the floor. Grinning, Vilstair snatched it up. She pressed it against her own jewel first, to make sure it held no viruses. When it came back clean, she pressed it to her temple, just below her own jewel. It connected to her brain, and she felt a brief pinch. Then the information came.

The jewel belonged to Madrigan Farovan, who hadn't been on any of the lists of convicts she'd seen. He looked Human, about twenty years old, and originally from Pirelli 3, a Neutral world not far from here. Four years ago, he met Geffin Chardan, who hadn't yet been sent to prison on Fronzesh, though he had already committed the crime which eventually landed him there. Over the intervening years, Farovan visited Chardan many times in prison, even bringing gift baskets. According to the jewel, he visited Chardan the last time a day before the first prison break. That had been six months ago. The more recent prison break came with Chardan (and presumably Farovan) helping from the outside.

She left the shuttle before she could glean more from the jewel. She could read more later, if she needed to.

Joranran knelt beside the robot, messing with its circuitry. The back panel hung open, and Joranran moved quickly as if he knew what he was doing. Butler watched the hangar while Vima leaned close to Joranran. "How did you learn all this?" she asked.

"Oh, I played a robot hacker a few years ago. I'm not one of those actors who just mindlessly learn their lines. We had a consultant who explained all the details for me, made sure I did the right thing during all my scenes."

Vima pressed her hands together before her, shifting even closer to Joranran, her eyelashes fluttering.

Vilstair marched loudly closer, hoping to stop the conversation before it got more annoying. "What are you doing with that robot?" she asked.

Joranran took his hands out of the robot. "Fixing it, obviously. It's one thing to chase thieves, Officer Bila. It's another to ruin their property. Besides, this robot did nothing to you."

Her headache refused to go away. As long as she had to put up with Joranran, she didn't think she could get rid of it. "I didn't ruin the robot. I hit it on stun. It'll come back on-line on its own. And when it does, it will alert the people we're chasing." She stared at him, unblinking.

He might be a good actor, but he didn't know how to take a hint. "Most stuns don't seem to hurt robots, but they can affect their mainframe over the long term. Robots are artificial, but that doesn't mean we should just abuse them." He stuffed his hands back inside to continue his work.

Great. A robot-rights activist. A robot-rights activist who thought Vilstair wasn't fully sentient. So, a machine built by people was better than a sentient creature whose birth had been aided by science?

If she hadn't hated Joranran already, she would have by now.

"If they give the robot its standard maintenance and updates, it will be fine." Vilstair knew far more about robots than he did, regardless of what roles he'd played. Her mind, unhelpful thing that it was, offered scenes from the holocin he mentioned earlier. She loved that holocin. Now she'd never be able to watch it again.

Joranran continued to ignore her. Vilstair turned to Butler for help — surely he at least had some sense. He was too busy glaring at a couple a few feet away and didn't react to her.

Rubbing her head — and how many times had she done that? — Vilstair turned to Vima. "I will require your assistance as I search the station."

"Me? Can't you go alone?"

"This is a formal investigation. Your assistance is not optional." Vilstair bit off the words.

Vima finally looked at her, though her gaze quickly traveled back to Joranran. Or, rather, Joranran's rear, which wiggled as he worked. "Let me call someone else. There are people who know this station better than I do." She tapped her jewel to make the call.

Vilstair managed to keep still and silent while Vima made the call. Her hands twitched the entire time.

"They're probably in the lower levels," Vima said, attention already back on Joranran. "Security will meet you there."

With a barely muffled shout of frustration, Vilstair stomped away from the shuttle. Of all the rude, unprofessional… She let the rant continue in her head for some time.

She stepped through the doors and onto the station proper. Shops lined both sides of the hallway, hoping to get money from people who had just arrived. People called out as Vilstair passed, offering her food, souvenirs, and cheap booze. She ignored them all.

She didn't need help to finish her mission. Thanks to the jewel she found on the shuttle, it would be easy to nab the thieves. Chardan and the others were on Farovan's contact list. She could call them if she wanted. More importantly, she could use her jewel to track theirs. Most people didn't have that capability on their jewels, but it was included as standard for Gray operatives like Vilstair.

Following the map her jewel provided, Vilstair moved deeper into the station. Soon, she left the areas filled with people. As the number of people decreased, so too did the lighting. She kept her blaster in hand as she moved into the bowels of the station. This had probably been intended as a holding area or perhaps cheap housing. Whatever the intent of the builders, now cobwebs dotted the corners and ceilings, and shady characters lurked in the shadows.

A perfect place to make illegal sales. Many Neutral places had locations like this; Vilstair had heard stories and seen pictures. This was the first time she'd ventured into such a place, and she wished for a partner. She could feel stares on her back, and she itched in anticipation of an attack.

A tap of her jewel transmitted her location to station security. If anyone was following as backup, they'd know where to find her. If. She grunted. She'd better have backup.

Everyone she passed kept their distance. As this was an official mission, Vilstair wore her uniform: a Gray jacket with orange stripes on the cuffs and collar. No matter how desperate or violent these people were, they weren't stupid enough to attack a Gray operative.

Finally, she got close to Chardan. According to Farovan's jewel, Chardan and three others from the crew were together, just around the corner. Vilstair put her back to the wall as she crept nearer. She heard voices.

"—and we're offering a fair price," a male voice said. Farovan's jewel identified him as Chardan. Vilstair eased closer to the corner, hoping for a look.

"It isn't the price that's the problem. I hear there are Gray paths after you," another person said. The jewel didn't identify that person: not someone from the crew of thieves.

Chardan huffed. "Even if the Gray is looking for us, that doesn't affect you. We won't leave a record of this transaction — not one the Gray can follow. You'll be fine, trust me."

At last, Vilstair could see. Four people stood on one side, three others opposite them. She cursed mentally. On her own, that was far too many to risk an attack, even with surprise helping her. And her backup was nowhere in sight.

She tapped her jewel, tagging the three people Farovan's jewel didn't know. They had jewels, as most people did. Vilstair's silently connected to theirs. Now, she could track them down as easily as she had Chardan.

Even if they didn't purchase illegal goods now, they were probably in the business. If she had time later, she could check the records for those three.

"Maybe," said one of the three buyers, a large Ulpilla with a red shell. They were the same one who spoke a moment ago. "I'm going to need guarantees beyond your word."

Chardan made an annoyed sound. Though gray dotted his hair and neat beard, he was a handsome man. He held up a hand and turned around, leaning in close with his three companions. The buyers shifted nearer to one another to also speak in hushed tones. Though the two groups watched one another, they no longer paid attention to anything else.

This was Vilstair's chance while they were distracted. Her backup wasn't here, but she had no idea when or if it would arrive. She shifted the settings on her blaster. Normally, it shot a narrow beam that only affected one person at a time. Like most Gray blasters, hers could be adjusted to make a wider beam. While it could then affect multiple people at a time, the effect wouldn't last as long.

That was good enough.

Without hesitation, Vilstair stretched her arm around the corner and shot. The wide beam caught all three buyers, who blinked, then crumpled to the ground. Chardan and the other thieves were just beginning to turn when Vilstair pointed her weapon at them. Another burst knocked those four unconscious.

All seven lay sprawled on the hard floor. Vilstair rounded the corner and shot both groups again two times, ensuring that the stun would last a few minutes. Then she reached into her jacket and pulled out a set of handcuffs. Fortunately, she had eight pairs on her. She had expected that she would have to chase down multiple beings.

She knelt beside the closest person: one of the buyers, not the Ulpilla. With a grunt, she turned him onto his stomach and then cuffed all four of his hands together behind his back. The cuffs connected to his wrists but also attached to his back. No matter how flexible he was, he wouldn't escape without help.

She quickly cuffed the others. One of the thieves was last. He began to stir as she secured him. With a nod, Vilstair stood and moved away from her prisoners, putting her back to a wall at a place where she could see down both hallways. She opened the com to the station's emergency channel.

"This is Gray Officer Vilstair Bila in section 4-EE. I have apprehended four suspects with three other possibles. Send security to my location immediately."

"Understood. A team will be there shortly."

She scoffed but ended the connection without comment.

Even though she had the jurisdiction to hunt down and arrest these thieves, she couldn't take them into custody without processing them with Waljik 6. She'd also need permission from the authorities to take the other three. When she checked on her jewel, all three of the buyers had arrest warrants for theft and purchasing of illegal artifacts. She'd known she should nab all of them.

The minutes passed slowly. When the seven prisoners began to stir once more, Vilstair stunned them again. They shouldn't be able to escape, but there were more of them than her. She didn't want to risk it. No matter how many stuns they took, they'd receive no permanent damage. Stuns were safe.

Finally, she heard footsteps. They came from the hallway opposite from the one she took. She relaxed for a moment, then stiffened because she heard only one pair of feet. A security team from Waljik 6 should comprise at least three people. She pressed herself deeper into the corner and gripped her blaster tight, ready to shoot.

A humanoid male came into view. Madrigan Farovan: both jewels identified him at the same time. He had a narrow face, large eyes, and skin that was almost white. Before she could attack him, he pressed himself to the far side of the intersection, keeping his body behind a wall. "You found us, officer," he said, voice echoing off the bare walls.

Vilstair glared and crouched, trying to get a clear shot of him. Where in the hells was the station security team? "If you turn yourself in peacefully, you will receive a lesser sentence." It probably wouldn't help, but she had to try.

A laugh came back. "Why would I do that? Everything's going exactly to plan. You found us a little sooner than I expected — you were able to hack that jewel very fast. No matter. You're here now."

Dread settled in her gut. She tapped her jewel, calling for the security team again. The sound of more footsteps came. For a moment, she hoped. Then she realized that they came from the same direction as Farovan. It could be the security team. If it was, they weren't broadcasting their approach. Standard procedure was lax in a place like this, but Vilstair couldn't imagine they would forget even that.

She could stay where she was, but there was nothing to shield herself with and nowhere to retreat. It would be a matter of time before Farovan and his fellow thieves defeated her.

She could retreat now before the other thieves arrived. While Farovan was already here, if she fired at him, he wouldn't risk shooting back. Not with his friends so close. She'd have to run, but she should be able to get away.

Or she could move closer and try to take Farovan out before the others arrived. That would put her closer to the wall, giving her cover.

The possibilities raced through her mind in an instant. None were good, but one was better than the others.

Keeping low, Vilstair launched herself forward. She ran in a crouch, darting left then right, shooting the entire time. Most of her shots went wide, but Farovan didn't peek around his corner.

Over the sound of blaster fire came more laughter. "Oh, I hadn't realized you were this good! This is going to be so much fun! We're going to Thlist."

Vilstair almost tripped. "What?" She made it to the wall, pressed her shoulder against it. Then she shook her head. There was something wrong with Farovan — maybe he was mad, maybe he was thick. It didn't matter, so long as she took him down.

She raised her arm, ready to shoot again. She had a clear shot, the wall no longer a problem. This close, she couldn't miss.

Her finger refused to move. Vilstair's heart thundered in her ears as she tried to move it. Still, her finger remained in place, less than an inch from the trigger.

She tried a different finger. Those also ignored her. Then she tried her other hand, but that didn't leave its spot on the wall.

Farovan leaned around the corner. "I wasn't obvious on Hreckin. You should be able to figure it out now. See you soon, officer." He winked, and everything went dark.

Vilstair collapsed to the ground, unconscious.

6

By the time Geffin met with their second contact, Madrigan had dropped away from the rest of the group. Polf stayed with him, but the others went with Geffin. It would look strange if Geffin met his contacts without backup. Since any of their contacts might try to betray Geffin, he needed the others helping him. With Madrigan at his side, Geffin never needed to fear betrayal, but Madrigan had other things to distract his attention.

The raid on Hreckin had made the news. The news hadn't learned any of the horrible secrets about Hreckin. Even the horrible things which were common knowledge, the news reported without rancor. "Hreckin is a recently established world," the anchor said, "Neutral as of three months ago. Its founders and many of its citizens are part of the Natural Birth Movement."

Natural Birth. Madrigan had to fight down the growl at the name. It sounded so nice, so pretty, that most people never realized how terrible it actually was. The people in the movement who only wanted to ban future Ill-gotten births were bad enough. Those that wanted all Ill-gotten beings killed or imprisoned or 'placed under observation for their own protection' were monsters. Madrigan's blood boiled every time he thought about them.

He wished they'd killed more people during their raid on Hreckin. People from the Natural Birth Movement had attacked a birthing facility on Ultremere just over a year ago. They killed dozens of children still growing as fetuses. All of the people from that raid had been from Hreckin. Some of the news outlets at the time reported that — the Gray news and, oddly, the Dark news. The Light, the Neutrals, and the official news from the senate didn't bother to mention it.

The Hreckin government had supported those terrorists, had helped them to plan their raid. They kept no records of that, and so no one could prove that they had. The Gray and Dark press included those allegations in their report, and the Dark happily put the blame for the incident on Hreckin. The Dark also congratulated Hreckin on a job well done, so their report hadn't helped much.

A year ago, Madrigan had hoped the incident on Ultremere might be enough to bring down Hreckin and the Natural Birth Movement. The only thing that happened was that beings in the Natural Birth Movement found it harder to operate on most worlds, moving the bulk of their operations to Hreckin. Hreckin's application to the Neutral was delayed; it only became Neutral three months ago. The five people who had caused the incident had been imprisoned on Diresi, where they would spend the rest of their lives. Beyond that, nothing had happened.

That was when Madrigan knew that, if he wanted to stop Hreckin and its horrible practices, he'd have to do something about it. He couldn't depend on other people, nor on the galaxy's various institutions.

Thank all the gods for Geffin. He knew what to do, and he had the resources to make it happen. It took a year for them to bring the plan together, but they had. There were no flaws in their plan. Hreckin would soon fall.

Madrigan lounged in a bar down the hallway from where Geffin met with his second contact. Geffin didn't want his contacts seeing Madrigan. While no record existed of

Madrigan's powers, Geffin still didn't want anyone investigating him. Madrigan was their trump card, the piece that made this operation possible. He couldn't be caught or suspected.

"When will the police get here?" Polf asked. They sat beside Madrigan at the bar, swishing their drink around and glaring at the nearby people. They sometimes raised a pincer in a rude gesture.

"It should be soon." The galaxy knew about the attack on Hreckin. According to the latest Neutral report — and theirs tended to be the most up-to-date since Hreckin was Neutral — an operative had arrived to investigate the incident. Nothing more had been said about the operative, not even whether the operative was Neutral or Gray.

Something strange was going on. Madrigan didn't know what. He couldn't hope to get a read on anyone from Hreckin, not at this distance. Certainly, no one on Waljik 6 knew: he'd already checked.

Not knowing made him nervous. Despite all his power, it was a feeling he knew well. The feeling never made him happy.

"You think this will work?" Polf glared at someone on the other side of the bar. They knew more about the plan than most of the crew, but they didn't know all of it.

Madrigan took a large swallow. He hoped the alcohol would soothe his nerves. Thus far, it hadn't. "It will work," he said with more confidence than he felt.

He opened his mouth to say something else when he felt a shift. Ever since coming here, he'd kept watch over the command staff of the station. It was always a good idea to watch the authorities: that was a principle which guided Madrigan's life. Whenever the Neutral or Gray operative arrived at Waljik 6, the command staff would be the first to know. Operatives always registered their presence with local authorities: it was standard practice with most of the alignments. It was far easier for Madrigan to track a small group of people who worked together in one room than to check space around the station, skipping through every ship to arrive.

The operative had finally arrived. Later than it should have taken, which meant he would have to be cautious. The woman was from the Gray, according to the command staffs' minds: an Officer Vilstair Bila from Diresi. A Gray operative meant Madrigan and the others had to be even more careful, but that their plan would have fuller reach when it reached its crescendo.

It would take her time to find Geffin and the rest of the crew. She would check in with the command staff first, which might mean making a stop at the command position near the center of the station. She would probably check the shuttle from the *Otteran* before she came hunting for them. All that would delay her, by as much as two standard hours by Madrigan's estimate.

If she came hunting for them immediately, they had minutes only. Madrigan doubted she would do that: not only was that dangerous, it went against protocol.

Bila was alone, as far as the command staff knew. That was strange: Gray operatives worked in pairs or more. Bila took longer to arrive than she should have. Neutral operatives were often unhurried, but the Gray could be trusted to be efficient.

Something was off here, and he needed to know what it was. Most people hated the unknown, but Madrigan took mysteries personally. He was saireishi — he was supposed to know these things, or at least quickly figure them out.

He reached out, carefully. Bila probably wasn't saireishi. The Gray had a number of saireishi, as did the Light and the Dark. Those were among their best operatives, sent only on the most dangerous or important missions. The attack on Hreckin wouldn't put Madrigan and the others in that category. Once the Gray knew who and what Madrigan was, that would change, but they wouldn't have sent their best after him. Not yet.

Still, he should be careful. Another saireishi would feel his power.

He checked the minds of the command crew to discover where Bila had berthed her ship. That gave him an area of the ship to check. When his mind reached that part, he circled it from a cautious distance.

He didn't need to touch each mind to discover who Bila was. Everyone in the vicinity was aware of her, watching her cautiously though pretending to be casual about it. Not everyone on Waljik 6 was involved in something shady, but the sight of a Gray operative made most people nervous. The Gray was allied most closely with the Neutral, and most people here were Neutral. Still, if the Gray arrested someone, even a Neutral, the Neutral would agree that the person deserved to be arrested. The Neutral rarely tried to argue with the Gray.

Carefully, Madrigan reached for Bila's mind. A brush at the edge proved that she wasn't saireishi. Good. His nerves calmed somewhat, and he slid closer to her, ready to dive inside her mind and discover what was wrong.

He missed her mind.

Blinking, Madrigan stared into Polf's patient face for a moment. Then he scowled and threw his mind back to where it had been. He hadn't missed his target since he was a child. It must be the nerves making him clumsy.

He came at Bila more slowly this time, knowing she had no defenses against him. Because he moved slowly, he had time to look at her mind before sinking into it.

Her mind was shaded, shielded in some way.

"Damn." Madrigan pulled back and considered her from a distance. She definitely wasn't saireishi, but she had protection from him. He had heard that Gray operatives were trained in basic, anti-saireishi tactics. Unless a person deliberately employed those techniques, they shouldn't be able to keep Madrigan out. No normal person kept up those tactics at all times. They were too exhausting.

Had Bila found a clue about Madrigan's nature on Hreckin, something which told her to be cautious? He didn't think he'd left any hints on Hreckin. Perhaps another saireishi could have detected him, but that saireishi would have then joined the hunt for him. Bila wasn't saireishi, and he sensed no other saireishi in the station.

If Bila had found a clue about him, she should have brought backup. She hadn't. Madrigan checked the other minds around her, and she was the only one dressed in the Gray uniform. Thus, she couldn't know what he was.

Perhaps the Gray had developed a new technology, something that could be worn like a jewel, something that could keep a saireishi out. Bila's mind wasn't shut off entirely. If he tried, he could still reach her. If it was technology keeping her from him, it was technology that hadn't yet been perfected.

"Madrigan."

He blinked as his consciousness returned to the bar. Polf gripped his shoulder, had shaken him while speaking his name. Instinctively, Madrigan did a quick search of the bar, looking for hostility.

He found it, two tables away.

Four men and one woman glared at him and Polf. They fingered blasters under the table, considering how they might attack. When Madrigan brushed against their minds, he sank inside easily.

Rumors spread around the lower parts of the station.

People whispered that the *Otteran* crew had come from a successful heist and were loaded down with all manner of treasure. That was true. Geffin had told their first contact as much in the hope of getting more interested buyers. Madrigan hadn't been happy at the time, but he hadn't protested. They needed an excuse to linger at Waljik 6, and looking for buyers was the best excuse.

This was why he didn't care for that cover. Greed ate at the five people at the table. They imagined all manner of things hidden in Madrigan's and Polf's pockets, things they could easily take. There weren't many people in the bar. The five weighed their chances against the possibility of being caught by station security. They hadn't decided to attack yet, but Madrigan thought it was only a matter of time.

He let his attention extend, beyond the bar to the area around it. There were no security guards in the area. Fuck. Of course there were never guards when Madrigan needed them. The closest was a two-minute walk away, too far to be useful for him.

He didn't want to touch the five directly. If he didn't take all five out at the same time, the remaining ones would be suspicious. If he did take them all out at once — because he could — the other people in the bar would wonder.

There had to be another solution.

Two women sat further away. They were looking at the five at the table and giggling. Madrigan tapped their minds. The women found three of the men and the woman good looking. They had already asked one another if they should approach the group. The last man, the one neither fancied and who was very muscular, had thus far kept them in their seats.

The two women had been drinking for some time. Not enough to be drunk, but enough to be more readily susceptible to gentle suggestions. Madrigan buffeted their courage. They were pretty and young. The last man at the table wouldn't hurt them. Even if he tried, the other four would stop him.

Giggling louder and clutching their drunks, the two women stood from their table. The five whispered instructions to one another, on how they wanted to attack Madrigan and Polf. Before they could form a basic plan, the women stepped between them and their targets. "Hello," one of the women said, holding her glass against her chest. "We were, ah, wondering if you wanted to have a drink with us."

The five suddenly had to deal with the two women. In the seconds when their attention got distracted, Madrigan slid from the bar, Polf behind him. He heard the five try to get around the women when they spotted their prey escaping, but the women were persistent. Madrigan grinned as he stepped out of the bar. He loved pushy women.

Once outside the bar, he and Polf walked quickly. While they could take care of any trouble that came their way, it was better to avoid it. They didn't need undue attention — not yet.

"Think you can send any pretty people my way?" Polf asked as they walked. They must have realized what Madrigan did. Unlike most of the crew, they didn't seem bothered by Madrigan's power.

Madrigan glanced sideways at them. He had avoided looking too deeply into the minds of any of the *Otteran*'s crew. He had to avoid Geffin most of all because he cared most about Geffin. It seemed rude to poke around the rest of the crew. Unless they did something to make him distrust them — as Shorvin had, time and again — he preferred to stay away from their minds. He caught strong thoughts and emotions but avoided the rest of it. While Madrigan didn't know much about friendship and camaraderie, he knew a few things. The moment he messed with their minds, they would be friends no longer. A friendship with a fellow saireishi could perhaps survive such a thing. As he'd never been friends with another saireishi, he didn't know.

The power differential between him and the rest of the crew was bad enough. Best not to prod it unnecessarily.

"You can get people on your own." He clapped a hand to Polf's shoulder, just missing the shell on their back. "You're good looking." That was what people did when encouraging one another. He'd seen it, both in minds and in person.

Polf snorted. "I'm not worried about my looks. It's my personality that's a problem."

"I hear there are people who don't care about that." He knew there were people who would enjoy Polf's personality. Sure, they were a killer, but some people liked that. Not just Dark paths, either. It might get more complicated if Polf wanted another Ulpilla, as that race of hermaphrodites formed large, complex relationships that Madrigan didn't understand.

When they next ran into an available Ulpilla, Madrigan made a note to look. Polf deserved a family.

Polf bumped their shoulder against Madrigan's. "You're new at this, aren't you?" Madrigan must have looked dismayed because they laughed. "Don't worry about it. You're good at it. Too good, really. I appreciate it, man. If you see any crazy people, point them out to me, yeah?" They clacked their pincers and wiggled their fingers. Both movements suggested intimate acts.

Madrigan had to put a hand over his mouth to stifle the laughter. "I will." Polf always made him laugh. That was why it was so important for Madrigan to keep away from their mind. If he touched Polf's mind, there would be no more laughter between them.

No one followed them or paid them attention as they moved further from the bar, so they slowed down their pace.

Madrigan reached out, looking for Bila.

She was on the move, heading deeper into the space station. Headed towards Geffin.

She must have tracked him already. Madrigan knew a Gray operative would be efficient. He tried to touch her mind again, but once more he slid off it. When he shifted again, he entered at an angle, trying to wiggle past her shields. He snatched a few stray surface thoughts. She knew where to find Geffin, had already checked the highlights of his criminal record. She had found the jewel Madrigan had deliberately left behind on the shuttle, and so she knew Madrigan's name too. Beyond her initial confirmation that he had no record, though, she didn't care about him.

"Are they here?" Polf asked.

Madrigan nodded. "A Gray operative named Vilstair Bila. She will reach Geffin soon." She moved quickly, none of the dim lighting or dangerous people around her giving her pause.

"Just one?"

"Just one." There seemed to be others. Madrigan nearly caught sight of two other people, but he couldn't get close enough to her mind to read details or names. They weren't Gray operatives: he got that much, because she'd been dwelling on it. Who they were, and why Bila had no partners, he didn't know.

One pursuer should have made him confident. Instead, Madrigan worried. If only he could see clearly into her mind. Then he would have answers his questions, and he wouldn't need to fear Vilstair Bila.

"Will we reach Geffin first?" Polf acted casual, but Madrigan heard the eagerness. Polf was ready to burst into action. There was nothing the Ulpilla loved more than a fight.

"No." He gripped Polf's elbow to keep them in place. "We can't run here. No one can notice us."

Polf huffed but kept their current pace. "No one can notice *you*, you mean." They didn't sound angry about it.

As he had many times before, Madrigan wished he could check. He understood Geffin's emotions without checking. His friend never bothered to hide how he felt, and they had four years together to back up Madrigan's conclusions. Other people were harder, even people like Polf, whom he knew better than most. He relied too much on his powers, like many saireishi.

When he failed to respond after a few seconds, Polf nudged him with their elbow. "Hey. Cheer up. We know you're the most important one here. That's why we aren't stupid enough to piss you off. Except Shorvin, but I think he might love Death."

Madrigan snorted. "Let's hope not!" The last thing they needed was a worshiper of Death in the crew. Geffin was fairly sure most of the crew were Neutral, but he hadn't asked. It wasn't polite to ask about another's beliefs.

As they approached the place where Geffin was meeting with his second contact, they slowed down. Madrigan reached out his thoughts. He still couldn't read Bila, he wouldn't read Geffin, and he preferred to avoid the other crew members, but that left plenty of other people.

Geffin's contact and his bodyguards were unaware of Bila's approach. Madrigan wished he could check if Geffin knew. Was he allowed to touch Geffin's mind if it kept Geffin out of danger?

Before he could decide, Bila attacked. Geffin and the others were distracted by their conversation, and Bila took the chance. She stunned them all, one by one in quick succession. Though Madrigan knew she was only stunning them, he couldn't help but pick up his pace. He was almost there.

When he reached the area, Bila had already handcuffed everyone she'd stunned and called a security team. No security team would reach this place in the next few minutes. The station tried to pretend that its lower levels didn't exist.

Madrigan slowed his pace again and nodded for Polf to keep back, just in case. There was something amiss with Bila's mind, and Madrigan didn't want to take chances.

"You've caught us, officer," he said when he stepped into view.

Bila raised her blaster and said something in return, but Madrigan missed it. Seeing her, he suddenly understood.

She was Ill-gotten, visibly so. Half-Human, as was typical of Ill-gottens. Human genetics combined with other species best. From her green skin, which had a moist sheen to it, the faint webbing between her fingers, the complete lack of hair, and the wide mouth, he guessed her other parent was Parleni.

He'd seen many Ill-gottens in his time, but never that combination. Anyone that visibly Ill-gotten must not have had an easy life. Her looks included both species, enough to make her unattractive to both. There might be a few beings who found her arousing, but likely as a perverted curiosity.

Her genetics explained why she'd taken so long on Hreckin. The people of Hreckin hated Ill-gottens, with an irrational prejudice. Even the people on Hreckin who weren't part of the Natural Birth Movement wanted nothing to do with Ill-gottens. That was the only reason anyone moved to Hreckin because it was the only planet whose government made it illegal to be Ill-gotten.

It was a wonder Bila got anything out of the Hreckin officials. Only her status as a Gray operative would have won her that much.

In all their time planning this operation, Madrigan and Geffin tried to think of every possibility. They assumed they had. Neither had considered that an Ill-gotten might be the one to chase them down. Though both the Gray and the

98

Neutral had plenty of Ill-gottens in their ranks, they were such a minority that the odds of running into one were very low.

For one wild moment, Madrigan doubted all of his plans. Did the Gray know about him, about his power? They might know. They might have sent Bila deliberately, knowing she had extra defenses against his power. She wasn't as dangerous to him as a saireishi, but she was the next best thing. While the Gray scrambled to get a saireishi here — because, while the Gray had saireishi, they didn't deploy them lightly — Bila would distract him and capture his comrades. It was a solid plan.

No, the Gray couldn't know about him. He'd been careful. He'd checked his records many times. No one knew he was saireishi, not even Capitania.

As he thought about what he should do next, he said something back to Bila. What he had said, he wasn't sure. His brain worked on autopilot. It offered something that would taunt her into recklessness. She hesitated, his words having an effect on her.

If she knew he was saireishi, she wouldn't have confronted him like this. She would take him by surprise if she could. If she couldn't, she'd throw distractions at him while attacking. No one with sense hesitated to attack an enemy saireishi. One might as well give up and die at that point.

Bila launched herself into an attack. She kept low, weaving from one side to another at random intervals, shooting constantly in an attempt to hit him. He stood close to a corner, using it to shield himself from her. He didn't need to look to know where she was.

She was good. Damn good. Of course she was good: she was Ill-gotten. The Ill-gottens that proved viable always ended up highly competent.

In that moment, Madrigan decided. Geffin might be furious with him, but they would go forwards with their plan.

"Oh, I hadn't realized you were this good!" he called. He made sure to keep the same taunting tone from earlier. "This is going to be so much fun! We're going to Thlist."

Bila screeched to a halt. "What?" Surprise oozed from her. She might be Ill-gotten, but her strong emotions still sang out to saireishi.

A normal saireishi might not be able to affect her, but Madrigan wasn't a normal saireishi. He had experience dealing with Ill-gotten. Their minds could still be influenced, assuming one approached them the right way.

Her moment of shock gave him the entrance he needed. He slid sideways, fast and precise. She blinked when he entered her mind. Likely, she didn't understand what she felt. Few beyond saireishi or Ill-gotten would even know that he'd entered their mind.

The waves of her mind rocked high and regular because she was Ill-gotten and because she was trained. It was a mind Madrigan wished he could spend more time inside of, if only he had the time. He hoped that she would follow him to Thlist. He wanted to speak with Vilstair again.

Her given name seemed natural now. He was inside her mind, admiring it and everything she was. After this, he had to be familiar with her.

When he reached out, the waves of her mind froze, as if winter suddenly settled over her mind. Her eyes widened, and he could feel her try to move her hands or her legs. As long as he kept her mind frozen, she was his prisoner. It might be harder to penetrate an Ill-gotten mind. Once inside, she responded the same way as everyone else.

Geffin is going to be furious, he thought. He spoke anyway. "I wasn't obvious on Hreckin. You should be able to figure it out now. See you soon, officer." With a mental twitch, he turned the temperature in her mind from freezing to boiling. The waves evaporated before they could crash down on him. Vilstair fell to the floor, unconscious.

"Nice." Polf appeared at his side suddenly. Madrigan jumped — he'd been so focused on Vilstair that he hadn't noticed Polf. Polf saw the jump, and smirked. "So that's how the mighty saireishi works."

"I was distracted." Madrigan tugged at the bottom of his jacket, pretending it needed to be straightened. "Come on, let's free Geffin and the others." He didn't wait for Polf but headed first to Geffin, even though other crew members lay closer to him. His first priority would always be Geffin.

The handcuffs had been keyed to Vilstair's jewel. Madrigan took her jewel out of her head with a soft, "Sorry," even though she was unconscious and thus couldn't feel it. Normal people couldn't steal jewels so easily, but Madrigan had never been normal. He inserted it into his head, on his left temple, since he had his normal jewel on the right. He touched each handcuff in turn, tapping Vilstair's jewel at the same time. They all popped open.

While Polf administered a stim to wake the others, Madrigan returned Vilstair's jewel. She had his extra. She knew enough that she didn't need it, so he took it back.

"I know you might be confused now," he whispered to her. She wouldn't hear his words now, but they would linger in her subconscious. He made sure of that, inserting them firmly. "You will understand later. Come find me."

"Fucking hells." Geffin came awake with a start. He pushed Polf and the syringe away, then grimaced when he saw the amount of grime on his clothes. This hallway wasn't the cleanest place to pass out. "You could have gotten here sooner," he said to Madrigan after taking stock.

"It will work out better this way," Madrigan said. He

didn't mention that he told Vilstair their destination. When he and Geffin were alone, he would tell him. They didn't need to make a scene here, not with other crew members listening in and station security a few minutes away.

When Polf finished reviving the last crew member, they headed towards Geffin's contact.

"Don't bother," Geffin said. At Polf's frown, he shook his head. "I know it's bad business, but one can't expect to evade the Gray. Besides, the Gray will need motivation to continue after us. Let's get back to the shuttle." He turned on his heel and started down one of the hallways, taking the fastest route back to the hangar.

Station security approached from different hallways, walking slowly. Though Madrigan kept an eye on them, he didn't have to interfere. He and the others made it safely back to the shuttle. As they walked up the ramp, the robot made chattering noises.

Madrigan sat in the first chair and examined the robot's log. He whistled at what he saw.

There were two other people working with Vilstair. They weren't Gray, weren't police of any sort, which was why she had seemed to be working alone. The Drilthin was a bodyguard and of no interest to Madrigan. The Human, on the other hand…

Madrigan distracted the people working in the nearby control station to keep them out of the way. Then he checked the face against the robot's database, just to be sure. Kyran Jorn, better known by his stage name Koyanran Joranran, was traveling with Vilstair. Jorn was from Hreckin, though he kept that quiet from the news. Like everyone else from Hreckin, he was scum.

Neither Vilstair nor Jorn had been part of his and Geffin's plans. They couldn't have anticipated the presence of an Ill-gotten operative, and they couldn't have anticipated that someone famous from Hreckin would accompany the operative during the investigation.

They hadn't planned for it, but it was better than Madrigan had dared hope. There were a few parts of the plan that were problematic. Madrigan could probably solve them with a cautious application of sairei, but now he wouldn't have to. Vilstair and Jorn together gave them everything they needed.

As the shuttle headed back to the *Otteran*, Madrigan laughed. They were going to succeed. In a few days, Hreckin would be no more.

7

Something prodded Vilstair's shoulder. She grumbled and shifted to the side, hoping it would stop. It came again, more insistent. "Officer?" a voice said. She swung towards the voice and connected with something. After a muffled grunt, someone tugged her off of her back. "Officer! Wake up!"

The volume finally made Vilstair open her eyes. "Wah?" She blinked and looked around. She was on the ground in a dirty hallway, four people wearing the same outfit around her.

Events caught up to her in a rush. With a gasp, she stumbled to her feet, knocking back the man who had gripped her. "What in the hells?" She had captured Chardan, three other thieves, and three buyers. She had cornered Farovan and should have been able to shoot him. Her body had disobeyed her, and then she passed out. There was no sign of Farovan, Chardan, or the other thieves. Their customers were still unconscious, their prone bodies placed on a sled that the security team must have brought with them.

"Are you injured, Officer?" It was the same Human who woke her up. His uniform was blue, with the logo of the Waljik 6 station on the left breast. He hovered just out of reach as if he didn't want to get too close to her.

She rubbed both hands across her face. "What happened here?"

"We hoped you could tell us that, Officer. When we got here a few minutes ago, you were unconscious. Other than those three—" he waved at the buyers "—there was no one here. I thought you apprehended more people than that."

"I did." She shook her wrists. No tingling sensation came, which suggested she hadn't been stunned. How then had Farovan knocked her out? Not to mention, how had he stopped her body from working?

A silence stretched. Vilstair watched as the other security guards finished securing the buyers on the sled. One man took the controls and pushed the sled down the corridor. It hovered about three feet off the ground, the perfect height for him to reach the controls.

"Why did it take so long for you to arrive?" There were far too many mysteries here. That one she hoped to solve quickly and easily.

The man winced. "Sorry about that, Officer. We came as quickly as we could, but there was a huge crowd in the fourth market, a few decks from here. We couldn't get through, so we had to take the long way around."

That was a pitiful excuse. Vilstair wasn't in the mood to argue. "Well, as my investigation involves other people, the Neutral is free to prosecute those three first. The Gray will take them if you want us to. Here's all the information I found on them." She tapped her jewel, transmitting the files to the man.

His gaze turned distant as he read the information. Then he sighed. "We've got lots of people doing illegal trading around here. I know the commandant wants to crack down on it, so we'll probably keep them. I'll keep you appraised of what happens. Do you require anything else?"

Farovan's jewel was gone. Someone must have taken it while she was unconscious. She traced where it had been. Probably Farovan took it. He told her that he planned to go to

Thlist. She didn't believe that, and anyway it didn't matter. While she had his jewel, she copied the information from that onto her jewel. She could still hunt the thieves.

Their shuttle had just left Waljik 6, moving slowly away from the hangar.

Vilstair clamped her lips down on a curse. "Show me the *Otteran*."

The security guard blinked, then tapped his jewel. An image appeared on the far wall. It showed Waljik 6 off to the left, plus the many ships orbiting around it. The *Otteran* was near the middle of the image, its engines alight.

As Vilstair watched, the shuttle landed on the *Otteran*. Before the hangar doors shut, the *Otteran* began to move. It turned, facing at an angle from Waljik 6. When the hangar doors shut, the *Otteran* jumped into hyperspace with a burst of blue lines.

"What in the hells?" The security guard slapped his jewel. "Control, what just happened? We have an investigation open for that ship! Why did you let them leave?"

The image of a woman appeared next to the picture of space. Behind her, Vilstair saw other people in similar outfits sitting at consoles. "The *Otteran* did not have permission to leave. I told them repeatedly that they would be committing a crime if they left. We were readying the tractor beams when the ship jumped. I didn't think they'd leave that fast. Jumping that close to a station isn't safe." The woman's hands clenched into fists as she spoke.

Vilstair stepped closer so the woman could see her through the link. "What's their trajectory?"

The woman glanced aside for a moment. "Thlist, Officer. That's a Neutral planet near—"

"I know where Thlist is," Vilstair cut her off. Without waiting for a response from the woman or the security guard, she turned and headed back the way she came. Her head ached, worse than if she had suffered a stun. She didn't think Farovan had done that to her. Not directly.

What were Farovan, Chardan, and the thieves playing at? Clearly, they wanted her to go to Thlist. Why? Did they have a trap waiting for her? There was no need for that. While she was unconscious, Farovan could have done whatever he liked with her.

Were they hoping that she would bring multiple Gray ships with her? Maybe the thieves had a weapon, something they hoped to turn against the Gray? Why anyone would be foolish enough to attack the Gray, she didn't know. Even the Light and the Dark, who were the strongest forces after the Gray and who hated the Gray, wouldn't pull an act of aggression for no reason.

"Do you know why they ran, Officer?" the security guard asked, voice soft, keeping pace with her through the station corridors.

"Not yet. I will. This won't reflect poorly on Waljik 6. Your assistance has been appreciated and will be reported. I will keep you updated on the chase. Now, if you'll excuse me, I need to leave." She gave him a quick salute.

Relief covered the security guard's face, both probably that she wasn't angry and that she wasn't blaming him or his superiors. "A pleasure working with you, sir. Please be careful for the next few hours. You were stunned."

She hadn't been stunned, which made it all the more important that she paced herself.

With a nod, Vilstair continued her walk back to the *Nebula's Edge*. When she reached the correct hangar, she didn't look for Joranran or Butler. She was hoping to avoid them. When she spotted the two of them waiting beside her ship, her headache returned, worse than before.

"You let the thieves escape on their shuttle." The

accusation slipped out before she could stop it. Maybe it was unprofessional, but she didn't want to take it back. Last she saw, these two had been right outside the shuttle. What in the hells had happened?

Joranran stood tall, looking down his long nose at her. "We only stayed beside the shuttle a few minutes longer than you did. Vima took us to the nearest control station, where we hoped to find the thieves. By the time we tracked them, they were already at their shuttle. There was nothing we could do."

In her work, Vilstair had heard lots of stupid excuses. As a student, she offered up a few of her own. Joranran's explanation still ranked as one of the worst she'd heard.

She opened her mouth but stopped short of saying anything. She remembered the way she couldn't move against Farovan, the way she collapsed for no reason. Something strange was going on here, something she didn't understand. Whatever had happened to her, Joranran and Butler might have experienced something similar. While Joranran was an idiot, Butler at least seemed competent. Throughout Joranran's explanation, he had a pinched look on his broad face.

He caught her staring at him. "There's something different about these thieves. We have to be careful. What did they do to you?"

With a scowl, Vilstair walked closer to her ship. She pressed the jewel next to the door, tapping her jewel at the same time. The door lowered. A faint hum told her the engines had started. Discussing what had happened with Butler might help. If he experienced similar things to her, maybe he knew what had happened. If talking with Butler also meant talking to Joranran, then Vilstair would rather go mute.

"Stay here," she said, pointing to the couch in the main

berth. "I have to make a report as we leave. It's to my superiors and *private.*" She said the last part with a pointed look at Joranran, who had already been headed towards the cockpit.

He huffed but sat on the couch without complaint. Maybe he'd been shaken by the events, too.

Vilstair closed the cockpit door behind her. As the ship flew slowly out of the hangar, she opened a channel to Yafan. He must have been waiting because he answered in a second.

"What happened? Waljik 6 said the thieves got away."

"It's insane." She tapped her jewel, transmitting a recording of the encounter. Since she was a Gray operative, her jewel recorded almost everything. After copying the recordings along with her final report, she deleted all of them from her jewel.

Yafan's gaze turned to the side as he watched the recording. When it came to the part where Vilstair couldn't move her hands, he bared his teeth in a deep growl. "What was that?"

"I don't know. I tried to move, Yafan, I really did. I couldn't. And I don't know how he knocked me out. He might have done something to Joranran and his bodyguard, too." Much as she didn't like them, the information was important.

"It almost looks like…" Yafan shook his head. "It can't be. It's not in our records."

"What?"

"You shouldn't leave Waljik 6 yet. Your partner isn't there yet."

Vilstair frowned at the change of subject. "The thieves are already on their way to Thlist. You want me to wait?"

"If there's a trap, then yes. Madrigan Farovan might be more dangerous than we realize."

"How can he be? The stuff he does, it's almost like he's a

lord." She clapped her lips tightly shut as a frisson of fear ran down her spine. The lords didn't hold all the power in the galaxy. Anyway, a lord would have better things to do with their power than steal from minor worlds.

"He's a Neutral, so he can't be a lord. I'm going to check. Wait at Waljik 6, Vilstair. Your partner should be there in a few minutes." He ended the transmission before she could argue.

With a few muttered swears to make herself feel better, Vilstair slumped back in her chair. She wished, more than anything, that when the mission to Hreckin came, she'd been on the other side of the galaxy. Then she could pass this mission onto someone else and not worry about it.

A knock came at the cockpit door. Groaning, Vilstair opened it. Butler stuck his horn inside, then the rest of his head. "Hey. Sorry about this."

"It's not your fault."

"I know." He glanced over his shoulder. "Being Jorn is wondering why the delay. We're far enough away from the station to make the jump into hyperspace."

"My superiors are checking on something. And another officer is coming as reinforcement."

Butler perked up. "That's good." When she scowled, he raised his hands. "I don't mean that you aren't enough, Officer. It's just, if we're tracking a saireishi, I want all the allies I can get."

Vilstair sat up straight with a gasp. "A saireishi? You think so?"

"Can you think of another explanation? There was no reason for us to follow Vima to that control station. Being Jorn wanted to spend more time with the robot, but Vima suddenly insisted. I told Being Jorn that we could track the thieves as easily from the hangar as from anywhere else, but he ignored me. That part isn't so unusual." He lowered his voice at that. Further away, Vilstair could hear Joranran talking to someone, but clearly, Butler didn't want his boss to hear this conversation.

She waved Butler into the co-pilot's chair. "So, what makes you suspect a saireishi?"

"When we got to the control station, I let Being Jorn go inside without checking it first. I never do that, Officer. There was no danger and only one other person inside, but that doesn't matter. When the door shut and I had to stand to the side, I didn't try to move. I couldn't see the displays from there, but I didn't care. I just... stood there. I stood there and didn't think about anything. No matter how hard I try, I can't remember if anything suspicious appeared on the monitors. The thieves must have gone right past the control station, so there should have been something. But I missed it!" He slammed one fist into the opposite palm.

"The thieves are Neutrals. They can't be saireishi."

Butler gave her a look that suggested she'd said something very stupid. "You think the Neutral is that careful with its people? You think there's never been an undocumented or rogue saireishi?"

"You and I aren't the ones who should be tracking such a person down." The Gray had a special unit to take care of such things, a saireishi strike team. They didn't lightly deploy. "Anyway, my superiors are checking into Farovan."

"Assuming he's the one."

Assuming there was only one. Vilstair shivered at that. One saireishi was bad enough, but two? Her hands itched for the controls, to call Yafan back and tell him to put someone else on this mission. She was fine leaving this to someone else. She remembered the way Farovan laughed at her, but even that wasn't enough to make her want to continue. Not if he was a saireishi.

A ship registering Gray dropped out of hyperspace not

far from the *Nebula's Edge*. It was a cruiser the same size as her ship, a standard design for Gray operatives. A com came through from the ship, and Vilstair patched through the image.

"Are you Vilstair Bila?" The image showed an identical cockpit. Two people sat inside: a male Chaukee and a female Human. The Chaukee spoke.

"I am."

"Ready your ship for boarding." The transmission cut off.

That wasn't polite. And she was supposed to work with one of those people? Vilstair closed her eyes for a moment. Really, the more she saw, the more she just wanted to be rid of this mission and everything that came with it. Proving that Ill-gottens were competent didn't matter anymore, not when everything else was going wrong. She wanted to go home and recover. Maybe she could even go to Writhim's funeral.

That thought made her wince. A long, complicated mission made a great excuse to miss his funeral. She was ashamed that she wanted to miss it, but she did. Though they'd only worked together for a short time, Writhim had still been her partner.

She shifted her ship to the side so that it floated alongside the other ship. The door could also work as a connector, allowing ships to dock in space. When the doors were aligned, Vilstair hit a button. The sound of machinery moving filled the ship as the cruisers connected with one another. Another button fixed the oxygen and pressurization. That done, Vilstair left the cockpit, Butler behind her. As they passed, Joranran looked up but didn't move. News from Hreckin showed on the display in the main cabin, which he must have been watching.

A control pad sat next to the door. Vilstair hit one more button, and the inner door slid open. The inner door on the other ship opened a moment later, and the Human woman stepped through. She was short with dark skin and white hair which tumbled down her back. She immediately made Vilstair feel inadequate.

"Operative Shinead Kielty, here to provide assistance." The woman saluted, a large pack on her back.

Vilstair returned the gesture by rote. "Operative Vilstair Bila. Thank you for your help." The niceties over with, she paused. "You should be aware, Operative Kielty, that we might be chasing a saireishi."

Shinead's eyes went wide. She clutched tight the strap of her pack. "No one mentioned that."

"We haven't confirmed it, but it's possible. Certainly, someone has powers."

"I'm here now, and I don't intend to leave. Besides, we don't have time to hesitate. The thieves must already be at Thlist by now."

Clearly, she'd been briefed about everything else. A beep sounded, from the other ship, indicating that it wanted to detach. Vilstair hit three buttons. The first put the inner door back in place. The second re-pressurized the ship and kept the oxygen inside. The third released the outer door. The two ships drifted apart, and the other one flew away and jumped back into hyperspace.

"Let's talk in the cockpit," Vilstair said. She waved to the side, indicating Shinead could leave her bag there. The *Nebula's Edge* only had three beds. She supposed someone could take the couch — not her, of course, since this was her ship. Not Shinead, as that would be rude. She wanted to put Joranran on the couch, but she was sure that Butler would take it.

Maybe they would spend enough time on Thlist to sleep there. Vilstair liked sleeping on a planet instead of a ship.

When she and Shinead reached the cockpit, the door

closed behind them. From the other side, she heard Joranran and Butler talking. Though Shinead had noticed Joranran, she hadn't reacted to him. Maybe she wouldn't be so bad.

Vilstair opened a channel to Diresi, and Yafan answered. "Shinead Kielty is here. Do you have anything else for us?" The *Nebula's Edge* drifted further from Waljik 6, far enough to make the jump into hyperspace safely.

"Thank you for assisting, Kielty," Yafan said to Shinead.

She put an elbow on the armrest of her chair and used that hand to prop up her chin. "We don't have time for chitchat. Are we chasing a saireishi? Are we jumping into a trap?"

Yafan winced at both questions. "At this time, we can't confirm either of those things, but they are both likely. Madrigan Farovan has missing records. We're working on finding out who he is, but we don't have anything yet. A team is being sent to Thlist, but they won't arrive for five hours. You need to go there and find these thieves. Keep a distance — a large distance. But you have to make sure they don't run again. We can't let these people go."

"Understood. We'll call when we reach Thlist." Vilstair ended the call, set the nav computer, and made the jump. The stars streaked into lines, and for a short time, she could relax.

Other operatives were coming to Thlist. Maybe the Gray hadn't yet deployed a saireishi strike team, but it wouldn't just be Vilstair and Shinead. That made her feel better, as did the order to keep her distance. She could do that.

"You're not afraid?"

Vilstair turned to Shinead. Though the woman hadn't moved, her expression looked pensive. "Of a rogue saireishi? Of course I'm scared."

"You don't look it."

"I'm Ill-gotten. You can't read my reactions."

Shinead snorted. "Of course I can. You're scared, but you

don't look it. You're Vilstair Bila, the being with the highest marks at the Academy a few years ago. I know how good you are."

The compliment, unexpected and much needed after the last day, made Vilstair duck her head. "Thank you. If you can get a read on my emotions, you're pretty good too."

Most people found Ill-gottens intimidating. At the very least, they couldn't read their facial expressions. Most of Vilstair's reactions were Human, as she spent so much time with Humans, but not all of them. And since her face moved differently, even those expressions looked different.

Shinead leaned back in her chair and offered Vilstair a too-sharp smile. "So, we like each other, and we might die together in a few minutes. Ready?"

The laugh escaped Vilstair, but she didn't mind it. There were worse people to die beside than Shinead. "May Order watch over us," she said.

Shinead nodded. "I'm hoping all the Gray gods will feel nice towards us, but Order is always the most dependable. You've got good sense, Vilstair."

"Not enough to avoid this mess."

"Life is shit — and by that, I mean our lives and the god Life."

Vilstair slapped a hand over her mouth at that.

Shinead quirked a grin but didn't stop. "You do what you can to avoid the nastier stuff, but sometimes we can't. We focus on the good parts and remember that we're making a difference."

Vilstair shook her head. No one insulted the gods. It was weird enough to find a Gray path who insulted a Light or Dark god, but one of the Gray ones? "You're insane."

"So I've been told. If you've been patient with that asshole in the back, then I trust it won't be a problem."

"No, of course not. I think I like your kind of insanity."

The thought of jumping to their death didn't bother her any longer. At least she'd had a chance to meet Shinead. She only regretted that they hadn't met earlier.

8

"This is not what we planned," Geffin said for at least the twelfth time — Madrigan had lost count. "You all but told the operative what you are!"

Madrigan leaned back in his seat, a smile playing about his mouth. In all their acquaintance, he'd never seen Geffin this worked up. Usually, Geffin had a plan, a backup plan, a backup to the backup, and then a few more possibilities if everything went to shit. Perhaps seeing Geffin like this should worry him, but it didn't. "The truth about me was going to get out soon anyway," he said. He'd said that at least five times already.

With a huff, Geffin crossed his arms over his chest. The *Otteran* was still in hyperspace, now less than a half-hour from reaching Thlist. Soon, they would have to give up the argument and join the rest of the crew. Geffin couldn't afford to appear weak before the crew. They would sense any moment of weakness and pounce.

"I don't like it." He'd said that about thirty times.

"It's only a minor adjustment of our plan. It will work, trust me. I'll make sure of that."

Geffin looked away from him. "I don't want to see you get hurt."

For a moment, Madrigan could only stare at him. How would he be hurt? Did Geffin really doubt their defenses against whatever the Gray sent for them? Madrigan was confident in his power, and he had thought Geffin was too.

If Geffin had feared for their safety, wouldn't he be angry or nervous? Without touching Geffin's mind, Madrigan couldn't be sure, but Geffin didn't seem that way. He seemed distant, worried. And he refused to look at Madrigan, even when Madrigan shifted nearer.

Suddenly, with as much clarity as if he'd read it off Geffin's mind, Madrigan understood. "When my history reaches the news," he said.

From the sudden tension in Geffin's shoulders, Madrigan had guessed right. "You don't like talking about your past. Now everyone's going to know about it. They'll never leave you alone."

Whom he had meant by 'they' was unclear. The media, perhaps, because the media would relish the story when it came out. The Gray certainly, because they would want to understand how it all happened and how to keep it from happening again. The Neutral, because they would want to ensure his loyalty. Officially, he was Neutral, but that was more from convenience than from any belief. The Neutral had no saireishi, and the thought of getting one as powerful as he would have them salivating.

"I am prepared to talk about what needs to be said." He'd thought about it many times over the years, what he wanted the rest of the galaxy to know. Terrible things had happened on Hreckin, not just to Madrigan, but to hundreds of children, maybe thousands. Even Madrigan didn't know an exact number, only that there were far too many.

He didn't like recalling those days. There was nothing good in those memories, only pain. He tried to pretend that he'd had no life prior to five years ago.

If it meant ensuring that justice was done to Hreckin and that no one suffered through what he had, Madrigan would talk until he ran out of oxygen. There would never be another like him.

"Do you want to ask about my past?" he asked. Geffin knew the salient parts, the worst of the horrors. He knew none of the details, had never asked.

Geffin still didn't look at him. "I care about your present and your future. Those are the important parts."

How Madrigan had found as good a friend as Geffin, he still didn't know. Maybe the gods had gifted Geffin to him as a greatly delayed apology for everything else he had endured. Geffin was enough for him to feel satisfied, but it wasn't enough for everyone else who also suffered what Madrigan had. They all deserved a Geffin in their lives. Since most of them were dead, they'd never have a Geffin.

"You're the only person I've ever cared about." He was far from the only one who had suffered on Hreckin. Any child raised like that couldn't help but be messed up.

It was his power that saved Madrigan. No one showed him affection as a child, but he soon learned how to reach out and feel other people. There was no love in the place where he grew up. The children couldn't love one another because they never met. They couldn't even meet one another's minds. The scientists found ways to mute their powers when they weren't practicing. It kept the children from overpowering the scientists and escaping. However horrible the scientists had been, they weren't stupid. One didn't lightly imprison hundreds and maybe thousands of saireishi children without plenty of security.

Madrigan had spent most of his childhood drugged or in fear. Both, mostly. His memories weren't very coherent. With his power, he could access his own mind too. After he had escaped, he looked back at his memories, trying to understand. When one child was tested, the others were drugged, and their inhibitors were taken down. If the child being tested, who was the only child not drugged or with

121

their power suppressed, tried anything inappropriate, the other children stopped that child. The scientists had a broad definition of inappropriate, and drugged saireishi children with no empathy were anything but kind.

Madrigan knew he'd killed at least eight children, possibly as many as twenty. He had been a child, drugged and terrified and not understanding what he'd done. Nevertheless, he knew he'd killed, and the weight of that knowledge never left him.

If not for that last child, that child who was so powerful as to make even Madrigan seem weak, he might still be there. He was one of the few experiments who survived childhood with an ability to control his power — and where he grew up, the latter was a necessity for the former. Children who didn't succeed were killed. They knew that and were reminded of it constantly. Most children despaired upon learning that. When they fell behind in their tests, they were then killed.

Madrigan used the knowledge as motivation. No matter how much they drugged him, he always yearned for freedom.

He still remembered the last day in the laboratory, the day when everything changed. He'd been in the practice room, training as scientists watched him.

"We're going to try something new," they told him. "Touch the mind of one of the useless children."

Useless. The scientists never hedged their words around Madrigan.

No child was born with sairei. To hear thoughts before one could form their own mind — that would drive a child mad. Most species gained sairei halfway through childhood. Earlier power didn't necessarily indicate greater power. Madrigan first developed power at seven.

The scientists bred children in the laboratory. They often expressed frustration at the breeding, the birthing, and then the caring for the children. Babies, toddlers, and children too young to show sairei had no value to them. They were a drain on resources, one the scientists had to endure.

During training, Madrigan touched the minds of normal people. He touched the minds of the other saireishi children. Sometimes he touched the minds of the scientists. He avoided the young children. It probably wasn't safe to touch their minds. He might ruin something.

"Well?" The scientists smiled at him. "Shall we get started?"

They liked to phrase things as questions and requests, but Madrigan knew better. He could not refuse. So, he reached out to the far wing of the lab, where the young children stayed.

He latched on to the first mind. He slid through the conscious mind quickly because he didn't want to see what was there. The subconscious curled below. Stacks of books rose to his right while images played to his left. Bits of string connected some things together, but many objects lay randomly discarded.

This child did not yet understand the world. They were still learning. Whatever Madrigan did would warp the child. Assuming he didn't accidentally kill the child.

He bit his lip. There were walls around the room, thick and strong. The child was young but already abused. This child already knew that only cruelty waited in the future. The walls indicated that one day, this child could defend their mind. In all likelihood, this could could one day be a saireishi. Maybe one day soon.

Not today, though. Madrigan nodded as he decided. He'd tell the scientists that he had tried but failed. They would have no way to know if he was lying. He had killed at least eight other children. He would not kill this one.

He turned to leave. A gray drape hung in place of a door.

Its edges fluttered in a breeze that Madrigan didn't feel. He stared at the drape, wondering what it signified. It hung between him and the exit, so he had to pull it aside.

Noise erupted around him. Alarms rang, bells chimed, and a cacophony of voices spoke over one another.

"No." Madrigan clutched the edge of the drape. It was too late. He'd awoken the child's sairei. He fled from the mind.

He returned to his body to hear screaming around him. The scientists doubled over or slumped on the ground. All of them clutched at their heads.

Madrigan didn't hesitate. He broke out of the training room and started killing. The security fail-safes triggered. That killed all the other children. That almost killed Madrigan.

He saved no one but himself. He thought a few other children had managed to escape, but he never tried to verify it, never reached out to touch their minds. He hoped they had, hoped that they now lived a life of joy and comfort.

Even before escaping, he learned how to latch onto other minds. During his childhood, he had to stretch far to reach happy minds, but he found them. Those minds had belonged to citizens of Hreckin. It made him sick, now, to know that he once found comfort in the joy of people who hated him. He had absorbed enough normal thoughts and emotions that, when he escaped, he knew how to integrate into normal society.

He spent his first month of freedom feeding off others, learning what made people feel and think. That was when he first felt guilt over the children he killed. That was when he decided to be a better person going forwards. That was when he decided he wanted revenge on all of Hreckin.

If he hadn't met Geffin around the same time, he might have gone off, frothing, to kill as many people on Hreckin as he could before he was killed. Geffin stopped that first, mad desire and replaced it with something cold and sensible, something far better, something which would work.

For that and for so many other things, Madrigan thanked the gods for Geffin.

He was pulled out of his memories when Geffin wrapped an arm around his shoulders. "You saved me too, kid." He spoke softly, even though they were alone in their cabin. "For the first time, I'm doing something good with my life. I owe you for that."

Madrigan could never picture Geffin as a bad guy. It didn't matter, his record or how many warrants he had. It didn't matter what Geffin had done in the past. He took in a young man who didn't have a heart and barely had a mind. Because of Geffin, Madrigan could be proud of himself. Because of Geffin, Madrigan was a whole man, not the wraith who walked out of the burning lab in Hreckin.

A beep sounded, and the com came on. "Boss, we're almost at Thlist."

Geffin kept his grip on Madrigan for a moment before he spoke. "We'll be right there. Ready?" He stared at Madrigan, eyes intense in the way he only got before something exciting and dangerous.

"Always." Together, they headed to the cockpit.

As they sat, Bakigan pulled the lever that dropped the *Otteran* out of hyperspace. Off to the right, a planet glowed blue and green with white at the poles.

Thlist was one of the most beautiful planets in the galaxy. Madrigan had visited here twice before with Geffin as they made plans. Each time, Thlist took his breath away. He wished that every inhabited planet looked like Thlist. If people lived somewhere beautiful, perhaps they'd treat one another less like shit.

Madrigan knew people at a deeper level than he would

have chosen. Beauty alone wouldn't fix the galaxy. If nothing else, his previous visits to Thlist proved that. There was just as much scum on Thlist as elsewhere. More, perhaps, because that type of being liked to prey on ignorant tourists.

He didn't pay attention while Bakigan spoke with the Thlist officials. Security was lax on Thlist. The planet was beautiful, but it had no valuable resources or wealth. As such, no one was interested in conquering it or raiding it. The local government did thorough inspections on ships before they left to make sure no one walked off with plants or rocks or seeds or anything else. That was the only major crime Thlist saw — unless one counted ripping off tourists, which the Thlist government didn't.

If Madrigan was in charge, he would have put more security in place. He was a paranoid person because he knew how often one being came after another. Thlist wasn't as safe as it liked to think it was. Few places were.

Unlike Waljik 6, they could land the *Otteran* here — or, as far as the local records would show, the *Oranteran*. It took Madrigan a month to forge such good records for the *Otteran*. He did it by tricking officials into thinking the *Otteran* wasn't already registered. As such, the second registration was in no way false. The frigate had two registrations, both equally valid.

They parked the ship in the capital city, on the south side where vast garages rose high into the sky. Since Thlist was obsessed with beauty, even the parking structures were clean, well lit, and painted bright colors. They ended up in a bright orange bay, which clashed with the *Otteran*'s pale green hull.

As far as most of the crew knew, this was their last stop. Geffin gathered the crew together to ensure once more that everyone had an equal share of the take. That took time since everyone had to empty their bags. They also had to count the money Geffin made on Waljik 6.

During the planning phase, Madrigan asked if this was necessary. "Of course it is," Geffin said, shaking his head. "I need to worry about my reputation. This is the last job you're pulling, but it won't be my last one. Anyway, I've seen it more than once, where crew members get into fights before they split up. I'm a good boss. As long as the crew is together, nobody fights. I have to enforce that."

Madrigan showed his share of the take, along with the others. Once the crew broke up, perhaps he could pass some of it on to Geffin.

"I'll contact you when I have another job," Geffin said once he finished checking.

With wide smiles and calls to work together again, most of the crew wandered off. Not all of them: Bakigan remained behind, along with Polf and a few others.

This was Geffin's main crew, the people he had known for years and trusted implicitly. Over half of them had been imprisoned with him on Fronzesh. These last few knew that the strike on Hreckin had only been the beginning of the true plan.

"Stay with the *Otteran*," Geffin told Bakigan once the rest of the crew was gone. Madrigan kept his focus on them, especially Shorvin. He didn't trust the other man. Shorvin might come back and cause trouble for them. "I want the ship ready to go if we get into trouble."

"Sure thing, boss." Bakigan offered a sloppy salute that made his antennae wobble. He then wandered back into the cockpit.

"You don't have to stay," Geffin said to the others. "I told you before that it would be dangerous. I didn't say how dangerous. Thanks to Operative Bila on Waljik 6, the Gray knows about us. They know about Madrigan, too. They won't send a handful of operatives against us. They'll send out an anti-saireishi strike team. You didn't sign on for that."

Polf glanced at the others. "I don't know everything, but I know a few things. And I know that you two wouldn't piss off the Gray for no reason. Why will the Gray come after us?"

"Because we're going to ruin Hreckin," Madrigan said, pulling the crew's attention from Geffin to himself. "Hreckin provides amnesty for members of the Natural Birth Order. Hreckin doesn't allow any Ill-gottens to work or live on their planet. That would be bad enough, but that's not the worst of it."

He had to pause and take a deep breath. He didn't want to admit this part, but he had to. Soon, he would have to explain to the whole galaxy. He needed practice with a small group of people who liked and trusted him.

"The Hreckin government and the Natural Birth order provided funds, a laboratory, and equipment for a group of scientists who wanted to do experiments on Ill-gotten saireishi."

"Ill-gotten saireishi?" Loddrin said, scratching his head fin. "I thought there wasn't such a thing." His gaze fell on Madrigan's pale skin. "Er—"

Madrigan continued. "They aren't common. As I understand it, the first few generations of experiments produced no Ill-gotten with power. It was only three decades ago that they first bred a child with sairei."

Polf made an aborted gesture, their expression strained. "Generations? Three decades ago? Madrigan, how long has this gone on?"

"Hreckin was first colonized around one hundred fifty years ago. As far as I know, the experiments date almost as far back. Obviously, the scientists in charge have changed. The Natural Birth Order is good at finding scientists interested in the experiment." Madrigan spoke without emotion. To him, it was an old, familiar story, one that no longer hurt, most days.

The other crew members stared in horror. These were terrible men, men who stole and hurt and killed. If even they found Madrigan's childhood horrifying…

"I'm sorry." Polf stepped close and gripped his shoulder.

That, strangely, made Madrigan feel like he might fall apart. He wasn't used to receiving affection from anyone other than Geffin. "Thank you," he said, looking to the side.

"I assume Hreckin kept all this quiet?" Loddrin asked, looking at Geffin. "Otherwise, the Light and the Gray would be all over them for child abuse."

Polf scoffed. "Never mind child abuse. The galaxy can ignore that when it's convenient for them. Everyone would be on top of Hreckin because they bred illegal saireishi — that's far more important to everyone."

"That is the true point of this endeavor," Geffin said. "With the laboratory burned down and most of the children dead, there is no evidence. It's been years, so I'm sure the Hreckin government has hidden everything that remained. While they must have erased any official records, I'm sure they still have something. Hreckin wants Ill-gotten dead or under their command. I'm sure they still have records somewhere, buried deep. If anyone went there, knowing about those records and looking specifically for them, they would find something. But we need someone with enough authority and determination. We can't do that, however much we wish to."

"How is having a Gray strike team come after us going to help?" Loddrin said, the scar on the side of his face twisting with his scowl.

Madrigan shook his head. "It will take at least a day after Vilstair reports for a strike team to reach Thlist. That gives us time. And she will come after us too. She has to — she's the nearest operative, and she has an edge against saireishi. She will get here first, and she will be the key to stopping

Hreckin."

Geffin made a face but didn't argue that. He didn't like Madrigan's revised plan, but he seemed resigned to it. "Will you stay with us a few more days?" Geffin asked. "We will need help to keep things working. I have friends on Thlist, but I trust you more than them."

"I've never been on the side of good before." Polk gripped Madrigan's shoulder again. "Might as well try it once."

"It's one thing to fuck people over, but children?" Loddrin shook his head. "Even we've got standards. That ain't right."

The other crew members nodded and offered their agreement.

Once again, Madrigan felt tears threaten. He hadn't wept since he was young. The lab on Hreckin punished weakness, and so he learned not to. He could stand terrible pain without crying.

He wasn't used to kindness and friendship. He had thought that he only had Geffin. Looking around the small group, he felt like the richest, most fortunate being in the entire galaxy.

I don't know if I like the whole Hreckin plan. It can work — Geffin's got a nasty mind when it comes to manipulating people. With Madrigan's help though, any plan can be successful.

The people of Hreckin deserve what they get. Scum, the lot of them. If the plan succeeds and the news shows how devastated the people of Hreckin are, I might want to wake up. If I can watch that, it will be worth waking up for.

Manipulating one or three people is easy. I've done it loads of times even when Yonaven isn't watching. But the Hreckin plan involves manipulating the whole galaxy or at least most of it. Some people will care but not everyone. No one knows better than me how little the galaxy cares. It will make the news for a few days. Maybe even a month, if the rest of the galaxy is being boring. Then people will forget. Even those who were part of it, those who cared the most, will eventually move on.

So long as it lasts long enough, Madrigan will be satisfied. So long as there is justice for the victims, Madrigan will be happy.

I'm not as nice a person as Madrigan. I don't care about justice for the victims. I want the guilty to suffer. I want their lives to be as bad as mine. That's impossible — no one's life is as bad as mine.

The people of Hreckin will suffer. It won't be enough, but I will have to settle. Madrigan is a good person. I'm trying to be better, to be more like him.

Yonaven hasn't been around as much lately. That helps. More than the people of Hreckin, I want her to suffer. I've debated with myself many times, what's the worse fate possible. I can't decide, which is why I can't decide how I want Yonaven to suffer. She deserves all of it and more.

Maybe I can learn a lesson from Madrigan. Maybe I can accept lesser suffering from the people of Hreckin. I can never accept that for Yonaven. If Madrigan knew, he'd understand.

9

"We're almost there." Vilstair watched the seconds count down. Two minutes until they reached Thlist.

Shinead worked the controls on the opposite side of the cockpit. With anyone else, Vilstair would have complained. This was her ship, and she didn't want anyone else messing with it. It didn't matter if they knew what they were doing. It didn't matter if she needed help. She didn't want anyone touching the *Nebula's Edge*. With Shinead, it didn't bother her.

"Shields at max, sensors up, ready to open a channel to Diresi or shoot our way back out." Shinead grinned.

With Shinead beside her, Vilstair didn't fear what they would find. Her hand on the controls was steady. The count reached zero, and Vilstair pulled the lever that dropped the ship back into normal space. She braced herself at the same time.

When no immediate attack came, she relaxed a little. Thlist hung to the left on her display, sparkling bright in the darkness around it. Ships clogged the area. Thlist was one of the most beautiful planets in the galaxy. Tourists came from all over to see its red fields and forests. Its desire to appeal to all tourists was the reason it was Neutral. Had it been Gray, few Light or Dark people would visit it. As a Neutral, it welcomed everyone.

According to the sensors, the *Otteran* was in orbit, currently on the far side of the planet. Shinead opened a channel to the planet.

"Thlist, this is Gray operatives Vilstair Bila and Shinead Kielty, here on an official investigation." It felt nice, saying their names together. Writhim had been quiet. Vilstair pushed aside the guilt that rose every time she thought of him and said, "You will give us all the information you have on the *Otteran*."

Silence stretched for a few seconds before a response came. "We would love to comply, Officers, but there's no ship called *Otteran* here."

"What?" Vilstair stared. Though it didn't show on the visual display since the planet was in the way, the *Otteran* clearly registered on their sensors. "Yes, it is! I can see it!"

"We have no record of that ship, Officer."

"Here it is," Shinead said. She hit a button to transmit the *Otteran*'s coordinates. "Or can't you see that ship?" She raised a pale eyebrow, her voice dry.

A snort came from the other end. "Of course I can see that ship, Officers. Your records are wrong. That's the *Oranteran*. That ship's been here many times. We know it. I'm friends with some of the crew, in fact." As the man spoke, a transmission came through, showing the ship labeled as the *Oranteran*. The transmission also included records that showed the ship visiting Thlist many times over the past few years.

"What in the hells?" Vilstair checked the records, but they looked legit. Their ship's computer found nothing amiss in them.

Shinead muted the com and said, "If Farovan is a saireishi, he could have messed with some of the people on Thlist. Also, there are ways to fake a ship's registration. Some of our people in intelligence can do that."

With a scowl, Vilstair turned the mute off. "Where is the crew of that ship?"

"Most of them are on the planet, Officer. If you want to arrest them, you'll have to show us your evidence."

"I already did." She sent that when she first opened the com.

"No, you didn't."

Vilstair pressed her lips tight to stop the scream.

'Saireishi,' Shinead mouthed. "Can we land?" she said over the com. "We can show you our records in person."

"Of course." Landing coordinates appeared on the display, and the man hung up.

"How do we chase a person who can change all their records?" Vilstair asked as she flew the *Nebula's Edge* closer. She had to go slow to wind her way around all the other ships.

"Unless he's lying." At Vilstair's look, Shinead shrugged. "The *Otteran* has been here many times. This might be their base of operations. They might have friends in the government. If I'd just killed a bunch of people and had Gray police chasing me down, I'd go somewhere I had lots of friends."

Vilstair rubbed a hand over her hairless brow. Her head ached again. "Or maybe they just think they're friends." A saireishi could do that.

"We don't know if Farovan really has any power," Shinead said. "There's tech that can do everything he's done."

"Is there? I know I wasn't stunned on Waljik 6." Disappointment knifed through Vilstair. This soon, and Shinead already distrusted her judgment? She'd thought they were friends.

Shinead held up her hands. "I didn't mean it like that. I know he didn't stun you. But there are other things he could have done. Maybe there were chemicals in the air. Maybe he drugged you. I'm just saying, we can't make any assumptions. Not without knowing more. Speaking of—" She opened a com line to Diresi. "Yaran, right? You know anything about this guy?"

Yafan's image looked worse than ever, and Vilstair wondered if he'd slept. His ears dropped, and his fur looked greasy. "It's Yafan, and don't pretend like you don't know." He bared his teeth at Shinead, who grinned. With a snort, Yafan turned his attention to Vilstair. "We've checked every record we can find. We were even able to access the records on Capitania. There's nothing on this guy. Not a birth date or location, not a school record, not a job history, nothing!"

"Is that even possible?" Vilstair said.

"Except with someone from a new or primitive world, it shouldn't be." Yafan let out a slow growl. "He must have hacked the system. Or created a new identity for himself. We can track him, but it will take time. I'm sorry."

"You should be," Shinead said and hung up. When Vilstair gaped at her, she sniffed. "He doesn't know anything, so there's no point talking to him. We know Farovan is dangerous. Let's just land."

Maybe she didn't like Shinead's type of insanity. Vilstair brooded for the entire short flight down to the planet's surface. They ended up in a parking garage on the south side of the capital, beside a hovervan with large windows along the sides. A man waited for them, his earlobes reaching down to his shoulders and his nose pointed far too high for a Human. An Ill-gotten? Or someone who had body modifications? Probably the latter. He didn't look odd enough for a second set of genes. A few guards and a robot grouped around the man.

Joranran and Butler stood next to the door, clearly ready to go. For once, Joranran wasn't smiling.

"We might be facing a saireishi," Vilstair told him.

"That makes it all the more important that I go. You wouldn't understand."

A day ago, she might have urged details from him. But now, she didn't care. The unimpressed look Shinead gave him made Vilstair feel better about her new partner. "Then let's go," Shinead said and stepped out the door first.

"Officers, hello. I'm Drinfer, minister of justice." The man glanced at Joranran and Butler but made no comment about them. "I'm sorry for all the confusion. The minister of the interior is a friend of some of the crew from the *Oranteran*, which you call the *Otteran*. The com officer you spoke with on your way down is also an associate of some of that crew. We can speak inside." He nodded to the hovervan.

They all climbed inside. The roof had a window too — the ship must be used for tourists. Probably every ship on Thlist was made for tourists. Even here, Vilstair could see the floating mountains in the distance. On any other world, those mountains would have been the main attraction. On Thlist, they were one of many.

"I received your records from when you first arrived here at Thlist," Drinfer said once everyone was seated. "The *Oranteran* matches the *Otteran*. I suspect that the crew has it double-registered."

"Never mind that," Joranran said, leaning forward and waving a hand. "Where is the crew now? Will you help us capture them and restore what they took?"

"That is where things get tricky. I and the ministry of justice are ready to assist, but many of the other ministers disagree. They say that the crew from the *Otteran* are our friends and that you won't understand."

With a tap of her jewel, Vilstair brought up images of the *Otteran* crew. "They killed four people on Hreckin, Minister. Whatever they've done for Thlist doesn't change that."

It sounded like the thieves used Thlist as their base of operations. Perhaps they had made many sales here. While few people lived on Thlist, they were all well off. This would be an excellent place to sell contraband goods.

If the thieves had established Thlist as their base, why first stop at Waljik 6?

Assuming anything would make sense with a saireishi involved.

Drinfer pointed at the image of Chardan. "He's a wealthy man and a good friend to many people here. Most people on Thlist will tell you that his imprisonment was unjust. I had heard that his sentence was to last longer than it did."

"It was," Vilstair said dryly. "He broke out."

"Ah. I see." Drinfer cleared his throat. His long earlobes wobbled. "I don't mean to be difficult, Officers, but there's only so much I can do. Please understand."

"If you want to help, then help." Joranran stood. Even though she agreed with him, Vilstair glared at him. He kept thinking he was in charge. Maybe they could ditch him with some local officials while she and Shinead tracked down the thieves.

Drinfer wrung his hands. "You don't understand. Capturing Chardan would be one thing, but Farovan? I'd be lynched!"

Finally, someone who might have information. "What do you know about him?" Vilstair asked.

An abrupt change came over Drinfer. Thus far, he'd seemed stressed and perhaps annoyed, clearly pulled between two of his duties. Now, his gaze turned distant as a calm settled over him. "Farovan is the hero of Thlist. He cannot be guilty of anything." Drinfer then returned to how he'd been before, stressing, "So you see, we can't apprehend him. Or at least I can't."

Vilstair and Shinead shared a look. "Farovan told me to come here," Vilstair said, thinking fast. "He wants to talk to me. Surely it isn't a problem if we just talk."

For the first time, Drinfer looked happy. "If anything else

happens, I don't need to know about it. Excellent! Yes, I can tell you where to find him. He's at the Capitol, along with most of his friends." Turning, he called for one of his bodyguards to take the hovervan there.

"Farovan knows you," Shinead said softly as they flew. The hovervan didn't go fast or high up, instead gently skimming the buildings. "He might know them, too." She jerked a thumb at Joranran and Butler. "He doesn't know me. I'll slip away when we land, see if I can take him by surprise."

"Are you sure?" If Farovan was a saireishi, they wouldn't easily surprise him.

Shinead made a cutting gesture. "We won't manage anything with this lot hovering over us. We have to try something."

"Very well." She didn't like it, but it was Shinead's choice. As a strategy, it made as much sense as anything else.

Maybe they could find a way to use Joranran and Butler as a distraction. Certainly Joranran distracted her.

The Capitol stood near the center of the city, a wide building with a large dome that floated on four tiny buttresses. It looked a beautiful, delicate thing, barely able to sustain its own weight. Vilstair's jewel assured her that it had been built with experimental, synthetic materials that made it perfectly stable but also allowed for its gravity-defying architecture. Buildings on Thlist weren't allowed to be merely operational. They had to be amazing, and this was more amazing than anything else Vilstair had seen thus far.

The hovervan landed outside the building, where tourists gathered. Guards and robots pushed the tourists back so Vilstair and the others could get inside. This was the seat of the Thlist government. That Chardan and Farovan could easily go inside didn't bode well. If the locals protested, they wouldn't be able to arrest the thieves.

By the second hallway, Vilstair glanced away for a

moment, distracted by a statue of a tree. When she turned back around, Shinead no longer walked at her side. Trying not to be obvious about it, Vilstair glanced around. She couldn't see Shinead. The other operative must have slipped away down another hallway.

Vilstair's nerves hummed. She couldn't help but imagine Shinead being stopped by a local official or killed by one of the *Otteran* crew or have her brain controlled by Farovan. Only by concentrating on her surroundings was Vilstair able to banish those thoughts.

Drinfer took them to a large room on the east side of the Capitol. No guards waited at the door. With a knock, Drinfer led them inside.

Chardan, Farovan, and a number of other crew members sat inside. They had drinks and snacks and looked like they were having a lovely time. Music played softly, and a screen showed the news. "Hello again, Officer," Farovan said the moment they entered. He had his back to them.

The door closed, keeping Drinfer's escort outside. A smile appeared on Drinfer's face as he casually leaned his back against the door. Like that, they couldn't get out without going through him.

Vilstair's heart began to race. She pulled out her blaster, though she didn't raise it. There was no point in shooting, not when she was clearly outnumbered. At least Butler had done the same — that made her feel better.

The thieves turned to Vilstair and the others, Farovan moving last. "Is this wise?" Chardan asked.

"We wanted to make a point," Farovan said.

"You are both under arrest!" Joranran stepped towards them, a finger pointed at Chardan's chest. "Give me back my things!"

Chardan snorted a laugh. "You think we're just going to listen to you? That's adorable."

140

Joranran's face flushed. When Butler tried to pull him back, he shook off his bodyguard.

"It's a trap, Being Jorn," Butler said, tone flat. "We can't do anything."

"I will not stand aside for injustice! You will turn yourselves in immediately! I don't care if you're a saireishi!" He said the last bit to Farovan, almost quivering.

Farovan said, "See?" to Chardan. "I told you they'd work it out. Everyone on Hreckin knows about his opinions — everyone in the galaxy who cares knows that he's an asshole. Having him here is exactly what we need."

Chardan didn't look happy, but he didn't argue. "As you say. We're committed to this by now. Hold on." He turned and tapped his jewel.

A moment later, an image appeared on the wall to Vilstair's left. She blinked as she recognized the background: the large atrium on Hreckin. She recognized the various decorations that abounded. A number of people gathered together, including Councilor Grisher whom she met earlier.

"Hello, Councilors!" Farovan's tone was merry. With his attention focused on the wall, Vilstair started to move. She shifted her feet slowly, careful not to raise her blaster. Though Chardan didn't look at her either, plenty of other people did.

Not that it would help if she got her blaster up. She could take down one, maybe two people before she got killed. Gray gods willing, Shinead was nearby, but she might not be close enough. Vilstair couldn't afford to wait. She caught Butler's eye and jerked her gaze to the door. Understanding crossed his face, and his muscles tensed as he readied himself to move.

"Madrigan Farovan." Grisher sounded disgusted. "I should have known you were behind this. What do you want?"

"It's not what I want. Being Jorn here wants to tell you

something." Farovan waved at Joranran.

Vilstair had only gotten two steps inside the room. Butler had gone further when he pulled Joranran away from Farovan, but they were still near the door. Drinfer kept his post in front of the door, but he was the only one there. And he, unlike everyone else, wasn't armed.

It felt like it took forever, but Vilstair had her body angled towards the door. One second was all she needed to get Drinfer between her and the others in the room. A lot could happen in one second, but Butler would move with her. At least one of them should be able to escape. Probably Vilstair because she wouldn't try to take Joranran with her. That was fine by her.

"I love Ill-gottens!" Joranran smiled widely. With a smooth jerk, he pulled his arm free from Butler's grasp. His bodyguard made a move to grab him again, but Joranran evaded him with greater skill than he should have possessed. Everyone's attention focused on Joranran, including Butler.

Sorry, Vilstair thought in his direction and launched herself at the door. Or she would have launched herself, except that her feet refused to move. They seemed bolted to the floor. When Vilstair tried to move, she nearly smacked her face on the floor. Only quick reflexes and a knee saved her.

Farovan was smiling at her. She had thought that she hated Joranran's smile more than anything else. Now she knew better: this smile was far worse. At least Joranran only had contempt for her. Farovan's smile said, 'I will use you until you beg me to stop.'

Joranran moved to Vilstair's side. His arm slid under her shoulder and pulled her back to her feet. Pain shot through her knee, but she ignored it. She tried to push Joranran away from her, but her arms no longer obeyed her commands.

"I've learned so much in the last day or so," Joranran said. It seemed to Vilstair as if his voice came from a great distance. Buzzing filled her ears, making it hard to concentrate. "This woman, Gray Officer Vilstair Bila, taught me. I now love Ill-gottens and her in particular."

So absorbed in trying to get loose and figure out ways to get her body to listen to her, Vilstair didn't notice the descending mouth until it was too late. Her eyes went wide and her mouth slack as Joranran's lips caught hers in a passionate kiss. Her instincts screamed at her to fight back, but her body relaxed into the kiss.

That made it worse.

Joranran pulled back after a second or three. A smile stretched his face, but disgust filled his eyes. He too knew what was happening. He too no longer had command of his body.

A cry sounded. Vilstair couldn't turn to look, but out of the corner of her eye, she saw Drinfer stumble. The door opened, knocking Drinfer further away. Shouts came from outside, accompanied by blaster fire and running feet. Then the door slammed shut, bringing silence with it.

"What in the three Dark hells?" Grisher said. He looked furious, with all four arms spasming. Beside him, a councilor bent over to throw up. Vilstair decided that was her least favorite person. "Ill-gotten don't deserve to live! They're an abomination! They're—"

"I'm withdrawing my fortune," Joranran said over him. "I'm gifting it to Madrigan Farovan. This has been broadcast across Hreckin and the rest of the galaxy. Now everyone knows that the Hreckin council is filled with prejudiced assholes. I won't be one of you, not any longer."

"You filthy—" Grisher was cut off when Chardan turned off the transmission.

Chardan headed out of the door, not glancing at Drinfer, who laid sprawled on the floor. "Where did he go?" he yelled. "Find him!" The door shut behind him.

Though Vilstair still couldn't move, she no longer saw Butler. He must have escaped the room, used the distraction of Joranran kissing her. She supposed that was a good thing, though she didn't much appreciate it.

When movement returned to her, she almost fell over. With a grunt, she shoved Joranran away and got a better grip on her blaster. Almost, she wanted to attack anyway, just to make herself feel better.

A moment after they separated, Joranran leaned over and threw up. "Gods, I touched an Ill-gotten," he gasped between heaves.

Vilstair's eye twitched. "Shut the fuck up, you asshole." She kicked him in the side. He groaned and collapsed, arms wrapped around his middle.

Farovan laughed and moved closer. "I am sorry about that, Officer. I didn't mean to degrade you, but something had to be done. We can't let people like Jorn, Grisher, and everyone else on Hreckin act like they're better than us."

"Better than us." Frowning, Vilstair finally took a close look at Farovan. Back on Waljik 6, she thought him humanoid, perhaps a modified Human like Drinfer. In the dim lighting, it had been hard to make out details. Even here, it was subtle, but it was there.

Farovan didn't have skin. He had scales. They were small and placed closely together, and thus looked like skin from a distance. His eyes were a little too wide, his nose a little too small. And when he raised his hand, Vilstair saw that he had no fingernails.

"You're Ill-gotten."

"Human and Flimlit." Farovan shrugged. "I have an easier time than you do." Flimlits had the same build as Humans on the outside, but unlike Humans, they had scales, larger eyes, and smaller noses. They also couldn't live outside water for any length of time — something Farovan's mixed

144

genes had clearly fixed. He also lacked the fins and gills that Flimlits had.

Vilstair moved further away from Farovan. Many people now stood between her and the door. She wouldn't escape. "You can't be Ill-gotten if you're saireishi."

Farovan sighed. When Joranran made another pained nose, Farovan scowled in his direction. "He should love you. He'd be a better person that way."

The actor slumped to the floor, loudly snoring a moment later.

With a nod, Farovan turned back to Vilstair. "You believe the lies that the naturally born tell. Ill-gotten aren't weaker, Officer. We're stronger."

"There has never been an Ill-gotten with power." All the records were clear on that.

"I'm the first. The things we think are true aren't always true. That's why the gods gave us brains, so we could solve the universe's mysteries by ourselves. A group of scientists spent decades doing experiments. I'm their first success. And my power is far greater than any other saireishi's."

Before Vilstair could respond, the door opened. Chardan and another man entered, both scowling. "He got away," Chardan said. "We'll find him. Where do we start looking?"

"Let him go," Farovan said. "He's no danger to us." Chardan looked doubtful, so Farovan clapped his shoulder. "He's not an Officer. He's Jorn's bodyguard. Jorn doesn't have his fortune anymore. It's ours. Once the bodyguard realizes he won't be paid, he'll leave. So don't worry about it."

Chardan scowled at Vilstair. "And what about her? Just because the two of you bonded doesn't mean anything. She still wants to arrest us."

"You killed four people on Hreckin!" Vilstair glared at them both.

"We killed people who didn't deserve to live," Farovan said. "You've met some of them. You know how they feel about Ill-gotten. Why should they live long and prosperous lives that are built on our suffering?"

Chardan said, "They've got Ill-gotten prisoners on Hreckin, you know. The gods know what they're doing to them."

Vilstair hadn't known that. Her gaze darted from one to the other. They might be lying. They were thieves and murderers. Just because they mocked Grisher and Joranran didn't make them allies. "If anyone on Hreckin is abusing prisoners, they will be brought to justice. You are private citizens. You are not allowed to kill."

The smile finally slipped off Farovan's face. "Then you won't be convinced?"

"I told you she wouldn't," Chardan said.

"My duty is clear." Vilstair held her head high. "I will hunt you down until either I capture you or I die." *Or unless someone else gets assigned this mission,* she added silently. This was beyond one operative, or even two. If anyone on Hreckin was performing experiments, that was business for the galactic senate. Even just taking down this crew was beyond her. They were too numerous, had too many powerful friends.

She could only hope that Shinead was fine and that she and Butler had met up. Even if Butler left, Shinead needed to know about this. Shinead would come for her. If not her, then the Gray strike team that Yafan said were a few hours away.

"That's too bad," Farovan said.

The world went black around Vilstair once more.

10

When Vilstair fell to the floor, unconscious, Madrigan allowed himself to relax. That could have gone wrong in so many different ways. He was still ahead. He could still win this.

"I'm glad you didn't kill her," Polf said. When Madrigan stared at them, Polf shrugged. "Killing Gray operatives is stupid. That's what got me captured. We're supposed to be the good guys here. We need to act like it."

Madrigan couldn't help the smile. Polf seemed alternately delighted and confused by their new role. They also had no idea how to act like a good guy, but Madrigan enjoyed watching them try. Polf hadn't killed Jorn's bodyguard, so they'd gotten one thing right.

Speaking of Jorn, Madrigan glanced at the man.

The actor slumped on his side in the middle of the room, a dippy smile on his face. He snored softly, lost to the dreams that Madrigan gave him.

Madrigan wished he could toss Jorn aside. The man's mind offended him. He wanted to keep as far away from that mind as he could. Even after having changed it, Madrigan didn't like it. Jorn's true emotions shimmered below the surface, waiting to bubble forth and show how awful he truly was.

Perhaps Jorn could be permanently changed so that he would never again hate Ill-gottens. Madrigan had no interest in making the change permanent. He would keep Jorn like this for a while — long enough to ensure that everything went to plan — then put him back. He wanted Jorn to see what his prejudice had caused, to fully reap what he'd sown.

It wouldn't be suffering enough, but it would have to do.

"Right." Geffin clapped his hands together. "There are some cells in the basement. Put Officer Bila there — gently!" he added harshly when Polf and Loddrin approached her.

"The Gray'll be pissed off whatever we do, boss," Polf said, more amused than argumentative.

"We're the good guys here, remember? We treat prisoners kindly."

With minimal grumbling, Polf and Loddrin picked up Vilstair and carried her out of the room.

"You should go help the others catch the bodyguard," Geffin told Madrigan. "They might need help."

The bodyguard was good. His name was Butler, an assumed name he took on when working. He was far more loyal and skilled than Jorn deserved. Madrigan had already taken Jorn's fortune and reputation away from him. Maybe he should take Jorn's bodyguard too. Jorn probably wouldn't care — and soon wouldn't be able to afford Butler — but Madrigan decided to do it anyway because even little revenges made him happy.

He reached out. It was easy to find the other crew members. Even though Madrigan had never looked deeply into any of their minds, he knew them. Their minds were easier to find than other minds.

Butler ran hard, taking abrupt corners, his mouth a grim line. He already had a com channel open to local authorities to report Jorn's abduction. That wouldn't matter — no one on Thlist would turn on Geffin. The few that weren't Geffin's friends, Madrigan would stop.

Butler had a destination. He was focused on it so clearly

148

that Madrigan didn't have to go hunting in his mind.

"There is someone else," he said.

"Who?" Geffin said.

"A Human woman. Another Gray operative, named Shinead Kielty. Apparently, Vilstair picked her up before leaving Waljik 6. They're newly partners."

When Butler had first met Vilstair on Hreckin, she had no partner. Jorn leapt on that, used it as an excuse to force himself on the mission.

Jorn had suspected why the *Otteran* had targeted Hreckin. He was a member of the Natural Birth Order and one of their best donors. Though he hated the idea of being stuck in a ship with an Ill-gotten — Madrigan touched those memories briefly, earlier, and just the thought of them made him want to punch Jorn — Jorn was willing to do whatever it took to keep the Gray and the Neutral away from Hreckin.

He tried to stop Vilstair on Waljik 6, but she had evaded him. Madrigan already liked Vilstair, but seeing the way she ignored Jorn on the space station made him like her more.

Butler had also been amused by Jorn's attempts. He didn't say anything, since he knew who paid him, but he offered Jorn no advice either. He might actually have been able to thwart Vilstair.

Though Butler had no interest in saving Vilstair — he felt a little guilt that she used herself to let him get away — he had to save Jorn. And he knew something had happened to Jorn. He had already told the Thlist government. Now he was on the line with the Gray high command.

And he was looking for Vilstair's new partner, Shinead. Shinead joined Vilstair before leaving Waljik 6, which was why Madrigan hadn't found her earlier.

They couldn't afford to have Shinead and Butler running lose. The Gray had been contacted about the danger. That wasn't a problem. Madrigan had anticipated that this would be the end of his obscurity.

He could handle the Gray strike team that came here, but not if he was also distracted by Butler and Shinead. "You might want to make sure about your friends here," he told Geffin.

Geffin made a face but nodded. "They won't betray us. I'll make sure of that." His tone promised all manner of nastiness if his local friends didn't agree. Madrigan knew without checking that Geffin meant it.

With a wave, he left Geffin behind with one more crew member as he went to help the others catch Butler — and Shinead, since they didn't yet know to look for her.

Butler wasn't a fool, and neither was Shinead. As soon as Butler escaped the room, he called Shinead. They were trying to meet up with one another — they knew that, individually, they couldn't stop Geffin and the crew, let alone Madrigan.

While it was a good plan, it wouldn't help. Being together meant it was easier for Madrigan to find them.

He couldn't easily find Shinead. He'd never met her, never even seen her. If he had time and quiet, he could find her. No mind could elude him for long, not while it was on the same planet as him. Shinead had likely also called Gray high command — probably also local authorities and Neutral command. She thought that, and the fact that she'd been hidden earlier, made her safe.

It didn't.

Madrigan followed Butler since he already had a tag on the Drilthin's mind. Certain species were easier to grab than others. Madrigan made no value judgments based on that — possibly he could just latch on to some species better than others. Drilthins were one such species. Now that Madrigan had him tagged, he could follow Butler anywhere in the galaxy.

Butler hadn't left the building. The crew members chased

too close behind him for him to give them the slip. He was aware too that a saireishi followed him. As a result, he took circuitous routes, made sure not to think too closely about anything. It was a good strategy, but it prevented him from getting far. That, and he didn't want to leave until he met up with Shinead.

Since the other crew members were far ahead of him, Madrigan didn't bother taking the same route. He took the lift to the ground floor and headed toward one of the side exits. Butler was nearby and getting closer, Shinead approaching from another hallway. They hadn't contacted one another in over a minute. They didn't need to since they had already decided on this as a meeting point.

A woman skidded around the left corner. She had dark skin and pale hair, was very pretty. She wore a Gray uniform and had a blaster out and ready. She noticed Madrigan and tried to do something.

She was too slow.

Madrigan grabbed her mind. Since he had to work quickly, Shinead stiffened. Her speed made her careen into a wall. Madrigan didn't like taking minds so quickly, but he didn't always have a choice. "Go to sleep," he said, pushing on that part of her mind.

Shinead slumped against the wall, the side of her face sliding down it. When she reached the ground, her breathing was slow and steady.

Noise came from the other direction: feet running, curses, and a blaster firing. Madrigan shook his head. He didn't want the crew to kill Butler. They were the good guys, so they didn't kill unless it was necessary.

Butler rounded the corner from the opposite hallway. He had his teeth bared, and there was a faint scorch mark on his right thigh: someone in the crew had managed to hit him. As he went around the corner, Butler shot.

No Gray operative would do that. Even though Butler had his blaster set to stun, he could still injure a person. If they stood near an edge, a stun could even kill them. Butler wasn't an operative, and he didn't care about that. He knew who was after him, and he was desperate. So, he shot without aiming, without being able to see.

It was a good plan, but it made it far too easy for Madrigan to avoid the shot. He ducked and snatched at Butler's mind. In seconds, the Drilthin was also asleep on the floor.

The other crew members appeared moments ready. "Thanks for ruining our fun," Loddrin said upon seeing both Butler and Shinead unconscious. He twisted his fin around and sniffed loudly as he put his blaster away.

Madrigan grinned. "Sorry."

"No, you're not. So where are we taking them? The same place as the others?"

Madrigan considered. He wanted to speak with Vilstair, a conversation that would be awkward enough without her allies nearby and unconscious. While he bore these two no ill will, they were his enemies. He felt no bond with them, as he did with Vilstair.

If nothing else, surely it was wiser to keep the prisoners separated.

He slid inside Shinead's mind. He didn't bother to be quiet, since she slept soundly. A check of her recent memories confirmed that she had contacted Diresi to ask for backup. She had reported that he was indeed a saireishi.

A Gray strike team was surely already on its way. While they would be interested in freeing Jorn and Butler, Shinead and Vilstair would be their primary concern. Madrigan couldn't separate all four prisoners; there wasn't crew enough to spread them that thin. If he put Butler and Shinead together, and then Vilstair and Jorn together…

Vilstair would be furious with him since she hated Jorn. Having him close might better prove Madrigan's point, though.

"Do you know the other building where Geffin set up?" he asked.

Polf nodded. "Yeah. He gave us the address earlier. You want us to take them there?"

"Yes. I'll stay here."

Two of the crew left and returned a minute later with a stretcher. It hovered at waist height as they steered it closer. Since it was narrow, they had to lay Shinead partially on top of Butler. They then strapped them both in, so they wouldn't fall out.

Polf lingered behind to say, "You shouldn't be alone."

Madrigan huffed. "I can take care of myself."

"No one's doubting your power." Polf considered for a moment, their pincers snapping softly. "You've never been in a situation like this before, have you? Needing to face an entire Gray strike team? Wanting to convince someone else that you're right? It ain't easy, either of those things."

He was prepared for the strike team. While he and Geffin planned this, Madrigan practiced the entire time. They always knew they wouldn't succeed without having to fight.

He hadn't considered that he might meet someone like Vilstair. She fascinated him in a way no one else ever had. Just knowing that he couldn't easily toy with her mind made a difference. If he tried, he could break into her mind. He didn't want to try.

He wanted Vilstair to agree with him because he was right. Perhaps she wouldn't like him because he and the crew committed theft and murder. She had to agree that Hreckin was wrong. That was the only thing that mattered.

"I'll be fine. Trust me. Besides, everyone else has something to take care of." He should be waiting for the Gray strike team. They would come from Diresi, or another planet deep within Gray space. That meant that the soonest the strike team would arrive was ten hours. Madrigan should spend that time readying for the fight. Instead, he wanted to use that time with Vilstair.

Polf shook their head. "Geffin needs to know about this. Maybe you'll see sense if he tells you to leave her alone."

Madrigan frowned. "Why can't I talk with Vilstair? She's sensible. She'll understand."

"In my experience, people are rarely sensible, even when you think they should be. You're young, Madrigan. You can read people, but you don't know people. And I don't want you getting hurt."

His frown grew deeper. "Vilstair can't hurt me. I have to try hard to use my power on her, but I can."

"That wasn't what I meant." Polf gripped Madrigan's shoulder. They looked like they wanted to say something more, but they sighed and turned away, going to join the rest of the crew taking away Shinead and Butler.

As Madrigan watched them leave, he had to fight down the urge to look into Polf's mind. Polf was his friend. Madrigan shouldn't read them without permission.

What could they mean, though, about Vilstair hurting him? It made no sense.

With a huff, Madrigan headed towards the basement. He didn't want to stop to talk with Geffin. Not when Geffin might be as weird as Polf. Vilstair would soon wake up from being put to sleep, and Madrigan wanted to be there when she did. Finally, they would have time and privacy to talk. She would understand. She had to.

11

The slow, gentle return to consciousness was becoming familiar. Vilstair shifted, only half awake. Her body felt loose and well-rested as if she'd had hours of sleep planet-side.

"I am sorry about this."

It was Farovan. She would always recognize his voice. The sweet lethargy fell away, and Vilstair sat up. She was in a small cell, a thin mattress under her. Farovan perched on a stool on the other side, alone. At her movement, he pushed a tray through the narrow slot on the side of the cell. Amazing aromas wafted from the coffee. Despite herself, Vilstair picked up the tray and dug into the nutribar. It was spicier than she usually prepared but in a good way.

"If you were really sorry, you wouldn't do this."

He sighed and ducked his head. "Maybe if I grew up like you, I could be kinder to normal people. You've had friends and family, people who accept you. I haven't."

"You get along with Chardan."

"He's different."

Vilstair sighed. Every criminal had a sob story and an excuse. This wasn't even the best one she'd ever heard. She took a moment to enjoy the coffee. Something sweet had been added to it, making it the perfect accompaniment to the spicy nutribar.

"I can understand wanting to change the galaxy. I can understand wanting to make prejudiced people pay for their views. I can even understand using me and Joranran." She resented it, but she would recover. "You can't kill people. No matter what they've done or what they think. The moment you decided to kill those people on Hreckin, you become worse than the people you want to stop."

"There will always be sacrifices. There will always be things you'd rather not do. You're Gray — you wouldn't understand. You think you can stay pure. If the Gray was more willing to do what it needed to do, it would be more powerful. You wouldn't have to share the galaxy with the Light and the Dark. They understand."

There were many differences between the Gray and the other alignments. The biggest, at least to Vilstair's mind, was that the Gray didn't mind the presence of the other two — or the Neutral or the Unattacheds in Capitania. The Dark didn't mind the other alignments, provided they submitted. The Light thought anyone who didn't agree with them was less. The Gray understood how to live with people of other opinions. The entire Gray alliance was built on very different gods, gods who chose to work alongside their opposites. Chaos and Order disliked one another, and Life and Death hated each other. They still learned to cooperate, under the direction of Fate.

"How is it you're Neutral, anyway? You're saireishi." The Neutral had no saireishi.

Farovan made a grimace of a smile. "Didn't you listen to my story? I wasn't born with official records. The scientists kept their work quiet. When I finally escaped, why would I go and register myself on Capitania? The last thing I needed was new masters."

"So instead, you decided to work with thieves and killers. That's much better." This was excellent coffee. She'd have to get the recipe out of him before the end of this.

As she leaned back against the wall, Vilstair let those

thoughts overtake her. She made them as loud as she could, far more important than their discussion.

"Geffin saved me. I know what kind of person he is. Thanks to me, he and his crew only target people who deserve it. The nutribar is setting 59-28, and the coffee is 808-34. I'll put it in your jewel." He raised a hand to show her jewel glittering dimly green in the middle of his palm.

Vilstair clutched at her temple, even though she already knew it was gone. She felt skin only. "If you hack that—"

"I haven't touched it except to take it out. I haven't even checked your contact list, I promise, even though I should. I'll put in the recipes and leave it alone. I swear it."

He was a criminal, and she shouldn't believe him. She was in no position to stop him from doing whatever he wanted. Even if she faked it, he was saireishi. He would pick up on her true feelings.

"Leave it where I can see it," she said.

"Fine." He stood and put the jewel on the stool, less than a foot from the bars. It would drive Vilstair crazy, being so close and yet out of reach. Bastard.

"How long was I asleep?" Without her jewel and with no windows, she had no sense of time.

"About an hour." When Vilstair frowned, Farovan offered a weak smile. "I am a powerful saireishi, Vilstair, far more powerful than you realize. Making an hour feel long enough to give you a good rest is easy."

"I see."

He had picked up her thoughts about the food right away. Vilstair had plenty of training, but she had never before met a saireishi. They were supposed to stay away from other people's minds, except in the case of criminals or when their own lives were in danger. Most saireishi were Light or Gray or Unattached, though. They had ethics and standards. Because of their great power, they were held to higher

157

expectations. Most saireishi relished that, honored that.

She should consider Farovan a Dark saireishi, as far as what he was willing to do was concerned.

However much he bragged, he had limitations. Butler had managed to escape from the room. A powerful saireishi should have heard his intentions the moment he constructed his escape plan. Perhaps Farovan had been distracted by his little charade with Vilstair, Joranran, and the people of Hreckin. That was the best way to deal with a saireishi. They couldn't read minds if they were too busy thinking about other things.

"I was hoping we could speak longer, but I can see that you aren't interested. Not now. Maybe, once you see what I have planned, you'll understand."

"I doubt that," Vilstair said.

"For now, I must say goodbye," Farovan continued, nose in the air as if he hadn't heard her. "Geffin and the others will need my help against the Gray strike team headed here."

Vilstair was on her feet and at the bars in an instant. Electricity crackled under her hands. It would grow stronger the longer she gripped the bars. For the moment, she ignored it. "How do you know about that?"

Farovan sniffed, his nostrils flaring. There was a hint of a gill on his throat, not fully formed. "I don't need to check your mind or your jewel for that, Vilstair. The moment you first reported my powers, your superiors in the Gray would have guessed what I am. It was only a matter of time before the strike team arrived. We've been counting on it, in fact." With a grin, he gave her a Gray salute and walked off.

She shouted at him, but it took only a few steps for him to reach the end of the hallway. The door closed behind him, leaving Vilstair alone. "Fuck." Her hands aching, she released the bars and flopped down on the bed.

Farovan and the others were going to kill the Gray strike

team. She was sure about that. There had to be something she could do, some way to warn them. They knew Farovan was a saireishi, but they didn't understand how powerful he was — and that he had no morals.

First, she tried to reach her jewel. When she slid her hand through the bars, the electricity ramped up higher. She pressed her lips tight, ignoring it. The bars were too close together for her to get more than half of her hand through. She couldn't reach her jewel. With a groan, she finally drew her hand back inside and cradled it against her chest, trying to ignore the pain.

All her equipment had been taken away, even her boots. She had her clothes and nothing else. The metal bed frame was fused to the floor and wall, and she couldn't budge it. The mattress wouldn't help her. There was a tiny toilet to the side, its controls outside the cell.

Vilstair turned slowly, inspecting every corner of the cell, hoping to spot something she could use. She found nothing. All the cameras and other monitors hung outside the cell, past her reach. Whatever else, Farovan and his friends weren't stupid. She hated smart criminals.

A closer inspection of the bars and the door showed no obvious weaknesses. As part of her training, Vilstair knew how to get past systems, but only if she had access to them.

Her gaze returned to her jewel. One thing Farovan said was true. Ill-gotten had certain advantages over naturally-born people, advantages which weren't well known. Many Ill-gotten weren't viable: they died before or shortly after birth. Only in the last century had science truly learned how to make such children able to thrive. Even then, some species combined better than others. When the scientists got it right, the Ill-gotten child often had the benefits of both species, which canceled out some of the weaknesses.

The electricity hadn't bothered her as much as it would a

normal person. Her hand ached and faint burns already showed on her palm, but it hadn't been so bad that she would scream. Vilstair had seen other people try to deal with the shock in cells. Most ended up writhing on the ground after a few seconds.

The Human half of her ached, but the Parleni half didn't mind. Parlenis were good with electricity — when they were incarcerated, they had to be put in different cells than other inmates, or ones with much higher voltage in the bars.

Even with her biology, she couldn't take the charge for long. And it didn't matter how long she could handle the pain if she could never reach the jewel. Vilstair crouched, tilting her head to the side as she considered angles, the gap between the bars, and the size of her various limbs. No matter how she twisted, she didn't think she'd be able to reach her jewel.

She grabbed the mattress from the bed, tearing into it. The fabric ripped to show the stuffing inside. It was loose detritus, offering little padding. Vilstair took a few handfuls out, braiding it together as she went. She didn't need much, just a few inches. When she had twice what she needed, she returned to the edge of the cell. One end of the braid she wrapped tight around her wrist. If she passed out from the pain, it wouldn't matter. Then, after taking a few deep breaths to ready herself, she pushed her hand through the bars and tossed the other end of the braid.

Sparks leapt into the air as pain arched into her. Vilstair pressed her lips tight and tried not to feel it. The braid was close to the jewel, so close. A twitch of her fingers moved it the wrong direction, and she nearly sobbed. Dark spots formed in her eyes as the electricity got worse. Blinking past the tears, she flicked her fingers the other way. The braid flopped, pathetic and still not close enough. It ended less than an inch away from the jewel, but that might as well have been a light year.

Spasms worked through her body. Even a Parleni couldn't handle this much voltage. She was still conscious, so she kept trying. Another shift of her fingers, and the braid moved again.

The dark spots overtook her vision. Vilstair drooped forward. That made her entire body press against the bars. The jolt that hit her pushed her back. She passed out.

When she woke, she found herself lying on the floor on the cell, feet spasming. It must have only been a few seconds if she could still feel the electricity. Vilstair tried to move her body but couldn't. She pressed her lips together and took slow, steady breaths, trying to calm down.

Finally, the worst of the pain wore away. With a groan, she shifted to her side, wondering what she was supposed to do next. Her gaze instinctively traveled outside the cell, and her jaw dropped when she saw it. The braid was still twisted around her wrist, all of it inside the cell with her, doubtless dragged inside during her seizures. She had reached the jewel, though. It no longer sat atop the stool. It laid on the ground, a hands-breath from the bars.

Vilstair wept, both in joy and because she'd have to put her hand through the bars again. Her left hand smelt of ozone. She didn't look at it because she didn't want to see the damage she'd done to it. When she reached out again, she used the same hand. If she escaped, she'd need her right hand able to move and fire a blaster.

The electricity felt stronger than before. Maybe it had been turned higher. Maybe her body could no longer handle the voltage, already weakened as it was. Whimpers escaped her, and she thanked the Gray gods that no one was close enough to hear.

Her fingers closed around the jewel, and the pain no longer mattered.

She yanked her hand back, so fast that she almost wedged it against the bars. Gasping and crying, she slumped back against the far wall, her treasure clutched tight against her chest. She had her jewel. Nothing else mattered.

It took a few minutes before she could do anything. Her hands refused to move, and her body burned. Finally, she used her good hand — the right hand — to pluck the jewel from the charred mess that was her left hand. She cringed when the jewel connected to her temple, re-establishing the link with her mind. The prick of pain didn't normally register, but it make her shake now.

As a Gray operative, she had a number of things on her jewel that normal people didn't. Sensors, large databases filled with information, and more. Her jewel could also could also inject a tiny amount of pain killers directly into her brain. It was for emergencies only, but Vilstair counted this as such.

The pain dulled immediately, and she sighed in relief. Then she shook herself and focused on the task. A tap of her jewel opened a channel to Yafan.

"The strike team is still an hour away, so be care— Vilstair? What happened?" His voice rose suddenly at the end.

She must look a sight. Vilstair managed a weak smile. "Farovan took me prisoner. Joranran too, I assume. He's Ill-gotten. Farovan, I mean." Maybe it was the pain, or maybe it was the pain killer, but Vilstair didn't make much sense. She paused to gather her thoughts. "I'm in a cell, somewhere on Thlist, I assume. Farovan is a saireishi and Ill-gotten. He has a grudge against anti-Ill-gottens. That's why he attacked Hreckin." That still didn't sound right.

Yafan nodded, though, as if this was a standard debriefing. "I will alert the strike team as soon as they come out of hyperspace. They're already expecting a saireishi."

"He's powerful, Yafan. They might not be able to handle

him."

Yafan's toothy smile glinted. It made Vilstair feel better — Yafan feeling his predator instincts was a good thing in her mind. "They've tracked down saireishi before. And the Gray has powered people too."

"We're awesome." Vilstair smiled at the ceiling of her cell. The Gray had many saireishi. They had the Admirals too, who had parrei, the best power.

"Can you get out of the cell?" Yafan's tone turned business-like. "Where is Shinead? Or that bodyguard you mentioned?"

"Don't know. Shinead went to look for a way to surprise Farovan. Butler escaped. Maybe he and Shinead are together." She hoped so. Maybe they could help the strike team when it arrived.

"Can you escape?"

Vilstair blinked a few times before she could focus on the bars. She had her jewel. Even without direct access to the wiring, she could now hack her way out of here. "Yeah. Give me time."

"I'll contact you when the strike team arrives. Be careful, Vilstair. If Farovan is a saireishi, he might know that you're awake."

"Yeah." Hopefully, other things were distracting him. Farovan thought she was secure. If he had to worry about other things, he wouldn't have enough concentration to check on her.

Wasn't there something else she needed to report? Fog clogged her brain, making it difficult to think. Most of the pain was gone, and she felt like she was drifting. Vilstair shook her head. She was a Gray operative, and there was something important Yafan needed to know. What was it?

"Yafan?" No response came. Vilstair blinked a few times before realizing that he'd hung up. He knew she was fine and working on her escape. He had other things to worry about, like warning the strike team and contacting Shinead. In other circumstances, Vilstair might have been annoyed, but the pain killer made her happy.

She giggled, then tapped her jewel to get it started on hacking the system in the cell. Once started, the jewel needed little input from her. That was good since the world now swam around Vilstair.

Her head lolled back against the wall, and she watched odd patches of color appear and disappear along the ceiling of the cell. She closed her eyes for a minute. When she opened them again, the colors were gone. That was unfortunate. She had been enjoying those colors.

A click sounded. Vilstair didn't move as the cell door popped open. *I'm free.* She pressed her good hand against her burnt palm. Pain lanced through her again, enough to focus her attention. *I'm free!*

Vilstair leapt to her feet. Rather, she tried to leap, and instead stumbled. Keeping her good hand against the wall for balance, she staggered out of the cell. There was no one else in sight. Had she actually managed to escape, even with a saireishi nearby?

As if in response to her thoughts, an alarm began to blare. "I had to think that, didn't I?" Vilstair kept close to the wall, moving as fast as she could. That meant no faster than a moderate walk. She was going to end up re-captured in less than a minute.

By the time she reached the door at the end of the hallway, no one had appeared, not even a robot. Had Farovan left her unwatched? Sure, he was powerful, but that was just stupid.

The door opened with a soft whoosh at her approach. A figure loomed from the other side, moving closer. Vilstair's eyes refused to focus and her body ached, but her training took over for her. During her Academy days, she complained incessantly, like most of the would-be operatives. Her instructor had insisted that she needed to be able to defend herself in any circumstance, even when both her mind and body were broken. He was right.

Damn him, Vilstair thought distantly as she crashed into the large person. Her arms wouldn't reach all the way around the person. She turned her shoulder into the wide body, reaching one arm higher and the other lower. A swipe with her foot took out one leg.

The person fell to his knees with a curse. Vilstair slipped the rest of the way around him. One arm kept him in place against her while the other wrapped around his neck, a prelude to choking him. That was as complicated as she could manage in her condition. It already made her injured hand ache.

When she looked down, she finally got a good look at him. It was Drinfer. It was because of him that she'd been captured. He had lied about not being friends with the crew from the *Otteran,* and then he physically prevented her from escaping earlier. With a growl, Vilstair tightened her grip on him. Not enough to drop him unconscious, but enough that he'd feel it.

"What is Farovan planning?"

"I— don't know." The words came out in two separate gasps. Drinfer tried to move, batting uselessly at her legs, but he had no training. Even as broken as she was, Vilstair held him in place. It helped that he clearly lacked strength.

"Where is he now?"

Drinfer tried to shake his head, and only succeeded in nearly choking himself. He coughed and gasped and said, "Waiting for the Gray. They're going to kill them."

"And you and your friends plan to help them." With the adrenaline from the initial fight drained away, Vilstair could feel her strength rapidly slipping. She couldn't afford to question him for long, especially since someone else was likely coming. The alarm had gone silent, but that didn't mean Drinfer was alone.

She exhaled and tightened her arm around his neck. Drinfer twitched for maybe three seconds, then slumped over, unconscious. Vilstair let him drop to the floor, then pushed him over to his side and took his jewel. The fun additions to her jewel meant she could do that. It had come in handy many times during her missions.

She inserted Drinfer's jewel into her temple, to the left of her jewel. Information poured out of it. There was no one else in the area. Drinfer had been alone, had turned off the alarm as he went to investigate. With the Gray strike team less than an hour away, no one else could be spared to watch over her.

That meant the *Otteran* had fewer allies here than she had feared. She had thought the entire Thlist government was working with the thieves. There were four other ministers involved in this, at least as far as Drinfer's jewel knew, but not all. That would help.

She opened a channel. Though she waited and waited, Shinead didn't answer.

Her heart sunk. Shinead must have been captured too.

She ached. Her hand burned, the pain killer made the world sway around her, and she wanted nothing more than to sleep. She forced herself to keep walking anyway. Shinead needed her.

She reached an intersection. Thanks to Drinfer's jewel, she knew where she was. Thlist didn't see much criminal activity since it had a small population and nothing easily stolen. The cells were mostly used for unruly drunks and people caught in domestic disputes. She was in the same building as before, albeit seven floors under the ground.

Drinfer's jewel had a complete map of the building, with

fire escapes clearly marked. There was a chute not far from her location, with a ladder that would take her to an underground parking garage. Her body cried out at the thought of having to climb a ladder, but it was safer than anything else. She couldn't afford to take the main stairs or the lifts.

A few feet from the chute entrance, she heard the faint buzzing of a robot. They made noise as they moved, a safety precaution so they wouldn't run anyone down. With what little strength she still had, Vilstair threw herself towards the door. She got it closed behind her just before the robot rounded the corner. She followed its progress with her jewel, panting against the ladder. It seemed to take forever to go past. Finally, with the robot gone, she groaned and started the long and painful climb up the ladder.

12

Madrigan forced himself to walk slowly as he left Vilstair behind. He wanted to weep, but he kept it together. He had years of practice, pushing his tears down.

Vilstair didn't understand. She saw the murder he committed on Hreckin and equaled it to the horrors the Hreckin scientists visited upon him and every other child raised in the laboratory. The two were nothing alike, the latter far greater than the first. Vilstair should understand that. Why couldn't she?

He wrapped his arms around himself. As soon as he was away from Vilstair's cell, he broke into a run. He didn't pay attention to where he went, but somehow, he made it out of the building, into the street, and to the other building that Geffin had prepared.

On the twelfth floor, he found Geffin and most of the crew. Butler and Shinead had been placed in chairs, restrained even though they were still unconscious. Images showed on every wall, monitoring the system, and Geffin and the crew debated how much time remained before the strike team arrived.

Madrigan took it all in through blurry eyes. He didn't care about the strike team. No one in the Gray understood. They would probably let the people of Hreckin off without punishment.

Geffin turned, his eyes finding Madrigan without

hesitation. His expression had been serious and thoughtful. As soon as he spotted Madrigan, he sighed and held out his hands. "Why did you talk with her?"

It didn't matter that the rest of the crew watched. Madrigan let Geffin pull him into his arms and hold him close. Geffin didn't often hold him since Madrigan was an adult and shouldn't need public affection. Geffin had to explain that to Madrigan since Madrigan hadn't understood when they first met. Madrigan had no affection in his past. Thus, when Geffin offered it, he wanted to take it, regardless of the time and place.

"I'm sorry," he said into Geffin's shoulder.

Geffin sighed, one hand on Madrigan's head. "I'm not angry. Not at you. I wish you hadn't talked with her. I knew she'd hurt you."

"How did you know?" Madrigan was saireishi, and he hadn't known. "She's Ill-gotten, like me."

"She's a Gray operative. They never understand. If a person is guilty of a crime — however righteous that crime was — that's all that matters." Geffin's arms tightened around him. "Most people haven't seen the crueler side of the universe. Grays and Lights in particular think that their gods are in control, that few bad things happen, and that those bad things happen only because their gods are trying to teach them a lesson. We know better. We know that the Dark is as powerful as ever."

Madrigan shivered. Geffin talked like that sometimes. However true it was, Madrigan didn't like to hear it. When he heard how Gray and Light paths talked, he wanted to be like them. He wanted to believe that there was love and kindness in the universe, that those forces were stronger than anything else. He had Geffin now and other friends. It should be easier to believe that than it had been as a child.

It wasn't. However far away he went, Madrigan could

never leave his past behind.

"A Gray strike team is coming," he said, pulling away from Geffin. The other crew members stood with their eyes averted, giving him and Geffin privacy. It made Madrigan love them all the more. "They'll be here in a few hours. I'm going to kill them."

The Gray would never believe him. The Gray didn't care about Hreckin and the Natural Birth Order. They thought Madrigan was the most terrible person around. If they were that foolish, they should die. Gray paths weren't supposed to be afraid of death. Having looked into many of their minds, though, Madrigan knew they were. Better for them to be safe in the underworld than messing up the universe further.

"No." Geffin grabbed Madrigan's shoulders, kept him from moving away. "We were only going to stop them."

"Why shouldn't I kill them? I'm already a criminal."

"You aren't. You've never committed a crime."

Madrigan had committed crimes. If nothing else, he'd killed one of the security guards on Hreckin. Geffin had a different view of crime than most people. Perhaps he didn't consider that a crime.

Madrigan looked first at Geffin, then at the rest of the crew. "They know about what happened on Hreckin. We told them, and Jorn and that councilor confirmed it. The Gray should be going after the people of Hreckin, not me. If they can't see that, they should be stopped."

Geffin growled. "We are the righteous ones here, Madrigan. I've never been in the right before, but I am now, and I'm going to stay there. We had every right to kill those people on Hreckin. They were as guilty as the rest. A Gray strike team? Maybe they are being foolish, but that doesn't mean they deserve to die." He shook Madrigan. "No one on Thlist deserves to die. You know that."

From the side, Polf said, "Except Jorn, you mean."

A noise escaped Madrigan, something between a snort, a laugh, and a hiccup. Trust Polf not to forget about Jorn. He was more useful alive at the moment — his fame and his confession would ensure that the entire galaxy heard about Hreckin. After they'd taken care of everything else, they could worry about Jorn.

"Except Jorn," Geffin said patiently, "no one on Thlist deserves to die. No one from the Gray deserves to die. They didn't know about the experiments on Hreckin. No one did. You were the one who said that we wouldn't murder the ignorant."

"Because we're the good guys," Madrigan finished. Their mission was a righteous one, but there were limits to what they could do in its service. Killing people on Hreckin was one thing. They all promised they would hurt no one else.

Geffin tightened his grip on Madrigan's shoulder for a moment, then let him go. "So you won't kill anyone on the Gray strike team."

"I promise."

When he escaped Hreckin, he thought most of the scientists who had experimented on him and the other children were dead. At the time, he hadn't checked, too overwhelmed by events. He hadn't returned to Hreckin until a few days ago, preferring to avoid it.

If someone had escaped the laboratory, they might have continued the experiment. Even if all the people directly involved had died, they likely had passed on their research information to others. The Natural Birth Order had many scientists in its ranks. Another person could continue the experiments or ones like them.

Because of that, the Gray needed to be strong. They had more interest in hunting down the Natural Order and its rogue scientists. The Neutral wouldn't care about stopping them, and they didn't have the resources besides. Madrigan didn't trust the Light, and no one trusted the Dark. The Gray was his best chance for revenge.

Vilstair didn't care about him, but he couldn't let her obscure his plans. He didn't worship the Gray gods, but he had confidence in the Gray's power and tenacity in finding criminals. Now that they knew, they would go to Hreckin. Hreckin would be punished, as would the Natural Birth Order.

He took a chair on the side of the room, resting while they waited for the strike team to arrive. Geffin and the others spoke about working with the authorities and the local police. Madrigan didn't listen. His mind drifted, focused on nothing.

Concentrating on nothing in particular, his thoughts stretched out. He soared high above, arching through the atmosphere and into space. Even he, the most powerful saireishi alive, couldn't reach beyond this solar system. He certainly couldn't find the Gray strike team while they were still in hyperspace.

He didn't know the moment to expect them, so instead he waited. When they arrived, he would know.

Many ships came and went. Thlist was a busy planet, seeing thousands of tourists every day. The local government knew the sort of trouble brewing on the planet, but even those not in Geffin's control would refuse to shut down travel around the planet. That would ruin their economy. And the Thlist government cared more about their economy than anything else. That was how Geffin got so many of them under his control.

That, and all the money Madrigan won for him over the past few years.

As it turned out, a powerful saireishi could make money extremely easily. While they spent some of it on obtaining the crew, fixing up the *Otteran*, and acquiring all the equipment they needed, most of it had gone into bribing various officials on Thlist. When a handful balked, Geffin told them the truth about Hreckin. Now, most of the Thlist government were their firm allies.

So long as they did nothing to harm Thlist — and they didn't plan to — their allies would stick with them.

He didn't know how much time passed while he waited. In his current state, it was hard to be aware of anything but the minds buzzing in orbit around Thlist. The ships that had ten or fewer minds on board, he ignored. A strike team would number at least a dozen. The strike team would be fewer than fifty, as they were elite forces. As such, any ship with more than fifty minds on board, he also ignored.

That covered all families and tour groups, as well as most traders. Madrigan only found a handful of ships with the correct number of beings on board. When one such ship exited hyperspace, he swam closer to it, sinking into the first mind he found. Learning a person's alignment was an easy thing. He only found one ship with Gray passengers, and that turned out to be tourists in a smaller group.

Regular Gray paths didn't concern him. They weren't even operatives, like Vilstair.

So he continued to wait. In this state, he could be patient for hours.

Finally, a ship arrived with twenty minds on board. Madrigan made a beeline for it, finding the pilot first. He was a Gray path, part of the Gray military. This could be the correct ship.

Speakers crackled to life, and a voice boomed out around the room. "Attention, *Otteran* crew. Stay where you are and lay down your arms. If you do not resist arrest, your sentence will be more merciful. Do not think you can escape us."

"Thanks for the warning," Geffin said. He didn't turn on the com, so no one on the Gray ship heard him. "Idiots. Madrigan?"

The pilot had already latched onto coordinates on the surface, a short distance from the building where Madrigan and the others waited. They had followed Vilstair, who was still in the cell in the government building. It seemed she had a tracking device implanted in her arm. Madrigan hadn't thought to look for it. Since Vilstair was harder for him to read, he hadn't realized she had it.

Still, he should have searched her mind more thoroughly before leaving her behind. If she hadn't upset him so much, he would have.

There was no time to regret his mistakes over Vilstair, not now. The strike team didn't know their exact location, but they could open a com channel to them. It wouldn't be long before the strike team found them.

According to Madrigan's research, the Gray had a number of saireishi among its military. Those saireishi were so different from Madrigan: they'd had happy lives, they served willingly, and they were without mercy. They were only sent out for the most dangerous missions. Any mission which involved hunting down a rogue saireishi would be considered extremely dangerous.

There were no saireishi on the Gray ship. Madrigan checked each person carefully. They had mental shields, the best that training and modern technology could manage. When Vilstair and Shinead first called for the strike team, they didn't know for sure that they were tracking a saireishi. For the possibility alone, the Gray sent out one of its crack teams. Since the Gray couldn't spare any of their precious saireishi on a possibility, there were none on the team.

That made it almost too easy. No mental shields could keep Madrigan out for long. No one on the team was even Ill-gotten, which might have made it tricky for him. He leapt from one mind to the next, sending them to sleep in turn.

As they noticed their comrades falling asleep, the

remaining members of the team grew alert. One took a stim — he lasted two seconds longer before he fell asleep. The pilot tried to open a channel back to Diresi to issue a distress call. Madrigan stopped him before he opened the line. The team leader tried to contact the local authorities. They might not easily turn on Geffin, but attacking Gray operatives was a major crime. Just like he had done with the pilot, Madrigan gave the team leader no chance to open the channel.

Less than thirty seconds after issuing their warning, all twenty beings on the ship slept. Madrigan nudged the pilot's quiet mind. He couldn't make a sleeping person do much, but he didn't have to. He had the pilot take the landing coordinates off, and instead put the ship into a wide orbit of the planet.

The ship couldn't land with its entire crew asleep. Not safely. And since Madrigan was a good guy, he didn't want anyone on the strike team harmed. Until this was over, they could orbit Thlist, out of the way and safe.

"It's done," he said to the other crew members, opening his eyes.

Geffin nodded. "They'll send another team when this first one doesn't check in. And the next one will be more dangerous."

The next one would have a saireishi. Maybe more than one. Madrigan knew he was powerful, but he hadn't tested himself against another saireishi since leaving the laboratory on Hreckin. And those tests had involved only him surviving.

They needed to finish their business here before the next strike team arrived.

I'm having a lovely time, watching Madrigan deal with a Gray path Ill-gotten, when Yonaven shows up. "Wake up," she says.

I cannot disobey Yonaven. I've tried. It doesn't end well. So, I open my eyes and look up at the dull, gray ceiling. Yonaven looms over me, looking down with a frown. Around me, she's always frowning. "What do you want?" I cannot disobey Yonaven, but I don't have to be nice to her.

"It's time to practice. Come on. If you try hard, you should be able to reach the palace on Gratevon."

"The palace is protected by the Dark Lord Timenar. I can't get past him." I roll my eyes. It's one of the few things my body can do.

"You haven't tried hard enough." She gets that impatient look on her face like she's constipated. She usually looks like that around me. She can do the frown-of-extreme-disapproval and the desperate-to-poop-but-can't look at the same time. Now that's talent.

I sigh, but I have no choice. I don't reach the palace on Gratevon. I never have, and I never will. I can get to other places around Gratevon, even get close to the palace. But I can't get past those walls. They glow. They glow black and blue, a glow that follows Lord Timenar around on the rare occasion that he leaves the palace.

I like Gratevon. Maybe because I spend more time there than anywhere else. Maybe because I know that will piss off Yonaven. Maybe because I know that everyone is a horrible person, but at least Dark paths are honest about it.

It takes over a day. That's long. Maybe Yonaven really needed some information. Maybe she got annoyed by me and made the training session longer as punishment — that's the kind of thing she does. That's what I thought at the time.

It's only later, after Yonaven leaves, and I'm free to go looking for Madrigan that I discover the real reason for the training session.

13

For the fourth time, Vilstair nearly fell off the ladder. One foot dangled loose, and she gripped as tight as her tired limbs allowed. To keep the world from spinning too much, she closed her eyes and pressed her forehead to the cool metal of the ladder. How much further did she still have to go? She was too tired to look up or down.

Hooking her foot back in place, she started climbing again. One, two, three more rungs: her mind, still high on pain killers, decided that it was important to count. She was at fifty-six, and she wished she didn't know that. Each rung came slower than the last, but eventually, she would reach the top. She hadn't been that far below ground.

She reached up her hand. Instead of finding another rung, she smacked into something flat, hard, and horizontal. For a moment, Vilstair didn't understand, still too sluggish. She shook her head and tapped her jewel. A green film tinged her vision. There were no lights in the chute, and this was the only way she could see. A round cover filled her vision, flush against the side and with no controls in sight.

"Please, Gray gods, open." She pressed against the cover. She might as well have tried to move the entire building for all the good it did. Her vision blurred as tears pricked the corners of her eyes. Vilstair rubbed the back of her hand across her face. "Stupid pain killers."

There were no visible controls, but she had her jewel. She

tapped it, and it went hunting. She held her breath as the jewel told her to stand by. Finally, she heard a faint click, and the edge of the cover popped open. The latch was on the opposite side, so Vilstair had to brace herself against the ladder and push with her shoulders. It opened, and she crawled out.

Noise filled the area. Vilstair was at the far side of a large room that teamed with people. Tourists, she guessed, based on their luggage. They queued to join tours or to take busses elsewhere in the city. She'd come out behind a garbage can, so no one noticed her.

She climbed the rest of the way out of the chute, closing the cover behind her. She checked the time. Seven minutes since she'd escaped the cell — it felt longer than that. The Gray strike team should be here at any moment.

She was free, but now what should she do?

First, a quick check of the room. No one jumped out of hiding, and she relaxed a little. She tried calling Shinead again, but still no response came. Though she hoped that meant Shinead was busy, she knew that wasn't true. Farovan caught her with ease. He must have gone after Shinead and Butler too.

There was nothing she could do for the strike team. They were surely out of hyperspace by now, and Yafan must have alerted them to the danger. Neither could she stop Farovan, not least because she didn't know where he was.

Various ministers from Thlist were helping Chardan and the other thieves. It sounded like they were friends with Chardan more than Farovan — Drinfer had only Chardan's contact information on his jewel. His jewel told her some things, but not enough. Clearly, Chardan and the *Otteran* crew had close ties with Thlist. Were the ministers here complicit in the murders and theft on Hreckin, or were they only offering a safe place to hide?

She had nothing better to do, and she ached too much to take on a difficult task. Since she was already in a government building, she might as well focus on Thlist.

As this was a center for tourists, there was a shop for first aid items. Vilstair tapped in her selection. The device didn't want to give her the powerful pain-reliever that she requested, but she was a Gray operative, so she got it anyway. A few seconds later, the items popped out at the bottom of the tray. She rubbed the cream into her burns, sighing as her arm immediately hurt less. While climbing the ladder, she had to use both hands, which made the burns worse. She wrapped a bandage around her left hand, tucked the rest of the cream into her pocket, and shoved the syringe into her inner elbow.

The pain soothed further. Some of the giddiness from the earlier pain killer remained. The better pain killers wouldn't scramble her ability to think. They were addictive, so Vilstair couldn't take more than the one.

Feeling better than she had in a long time, she made her way through the center, keeping to the side. The tourists seemed calm. Surely, if a Gray ship had been blown up in orbit, people would panic. Ships getting blown up was bad for business, so maybe Farovan made something more subtle happen to the strike team. Or maybe Shinead had already stopped him. Vilstair could hope that.

When she reached the far side of the room, she was about to leave. Then she spotted a familiar form from the corner of her eye. "Oh, hells no." She turned, hoping she was mistaken.

She wasn't. There was Joranran, smiling widely at the young men and women clustered around him. He laughed and posed with them, looking like he didn't have a care in the world.

Despite herself, Vilstair approached. He looked fine. Farovan hadn't visibly hurt him, but surely having one's mind altered so severely should cause distress. He was an actor — maybe he was faking his cheer.

He looked up and spotted her. Vilstair cursed silently, but Joranran grinned. "Vilstair, darling! Come here!"

"Darling?"

"Everyone, this is my lover, Vilstair Bila!" His groupies all stared at Vilstair, many of them openly jealous.

Heat rushed to her face. "We are not lovers!"

"We're in love!" The crowd parted to let Joranran through. Before Vilstair thought to escape, he was beside her, his arm wrapping around her shoulders. Her elbows itched with the desire to push him off her by force, but Vilstair restrained herself. She couldn't be rude in public — it would reflect badly on the Gray.

Instead, she ducked under his arm, pivoted, and took off at an angle. The stupid man called out her name and hurried after her. She felt his hand brush against her back a few times, which only increased her pace.

Farovan changed him. Thanks to him, Joranran loved her. Couldn't he have made Joranran love her from a distance? She pressed her lips together, trying to hold in her anger.

When she reached the door, she turned towards a deserted hallway. Joranran kept up with her. As quiet descended around them, Vilstair stopped and whirled on him.

"Vilstair? What's wrong?" His expression looked so hurt.

"What the fuck is your problem?" Her voice echoed off the bare walls, but Vilstair refused to moderate her tone. She'd put up with far too much shit already. "We are not lovers. We are not even friends. Leave me alone." One person crossed at the end of the corridor, turning to stare at them. Vilstair wished she could just stun Joranran and be free of him. Stupid need to not make the Gray look bad.

"Vilstair." Surely no one should be able to sound that pathetic, especially not someone she disliked so much. Joranran went down to one knee, both hands extended towards her. "I know I haven't always been perfect. I know I've made mistakes, and I know that I treated you badly when we first met. I know I misspoke just now. I've been so consumed by my love for you that I said something I shouldn't. Forgive me, please? I will try to be better in the future, I promise."

She couldn't look at him. Vilstair turned, rubbing the ache between her temples. More than anything, she wished for more pain killers. That wouldn't make Joranran go away, but she'd be too drugged up to be annoyed.

Forgiveness wasn't a Gray tenant. Penance was. A person should be given a chance to serve penance and change their behavior. If they proved that they could do better, they should then be forgiven for their previous mistakes.

He was a celebrity, and she needed to question some of the local officials. He might be useful. Gray gods, but she wished that wasn't the case.

"Do you know any of the ministers here on Thlist?"

He blinked at her question and tapped his jewel. "Not well, but I've met the Assistant Prime Minister on a number of occasions. She loves my holocins."

"She's a woman. Of course she does." Damn, her headache had only gotten worse. She didn't have many other resources at the moment, and she still hadn't heard back from Shinead or Yafan. "Can you get us a meeting with her? Now?"

"I'll try." His smile far too wide, Joranran jumped to his feet. He tapped his jewel and turned aside as he made the call. Had he not noticed that she hadn't forgiven him? Or did he not care? If he was waiting for forgiveness, he would need lots of patience. Even if he proved a better partner than

Shinead, Vilstair would never forget the things he'd said or done.

Anyway, he hadn't really changed his mind. Farovan changed it for him.

"Minister Chikkit is available now," Joranran said when he ended his call. "Her office is this way." He headed down a side corridor, not waiting for Vilstair.

Gray gods, even when he tried to be nice, he was still an ass. Vilstair pressed her lips together and followed. At least the worst of the pain had faded in her hand. She wouldn't be able to use a blaster with it or do much of anything else, but the lack of pain was wonderful.

"My first wife was Ill-gotten, you know," Joranran said as he headed towards an elevator.

"I don't care." She hadn't known that. Admittedly, she wasn't a celebrity stalker who lapped up every tidbit of news or gossip. She thought he was married — he had definitely been married at some point. Back during her Academy days, she followed that sort of thing far more closely.

"It was from before I became famous. It was a terrible marriage, and she almost ruined my career." Joranran stared at her during the ride in the lift. "I hated her family too. I blamed all Ill-gottens because a few of them were rude to me. I'm sorry. I understand now how wrong I was."

When the lift doors opened, Vilstair made sure she got off first. "I don't care." Joranran could be prejudiced against whomever he liked. Soon, she wouldn't have to worry about him anymore.

Minister Chikkit had her office halfway down the hallway. A robot stood guard, but no one else. Thlist was a safe world that probably didn't employ much sentient security. Though the door stood ajar, Vilstair knocked on the frame.

Joranran, far less polite, pushed the door open and

184

stepped inside. "Hello, Assistant Prime Minister!" His smile blinded.

A short Huckfering woman sat at a desk, her fur a grayed brown. Her eyes and ears perked up at Joranran's entrance, and she clasped both paws over her chest. "Koyanran Joranran! Please, come in!" She hopped to her feet and scurried over to the drink machine on the wall. She returned a moment later with a steaming cup of tea. When she placed it in front of Joranran, she made a shallow curtsy.

Vilstair felt ill. She didn't bother with the other chair, instead placing both hands on the desk and leaning close so that she loomed over the Huckfering. "Assistant Prime Minister Chikkit, I am Gray Officer Vilstair Bila. I need to ask you some questions and then check your jewel and your records."

The woman looked between Vilstair and Joranran, her eyes wide and ears down-turned. "Is there a problem, Officer? I heard there's a Gray strike team coming, but they haven't landed yet."

"Have there been any attacks in the system?" When Vilstair tapped the jewel she had taken from Drinfer, she saw no news about an attack. Unless someone had shut down his jewel, and all the tourists' jewels, that meant no shots had been fired.

"Nothing, no," Chikkit said.

There had been no attacks, but that didn't mean the strike team was fine. They hadn't landed yet; they should have.

She tried to call again, Shinead, Butler, and any Gray ships in the system. No one replied. Her stomach twisted itself into knots as she turned her attention back to Chikkit. She could do nothing to help the others since she didn't even know where they were. Instead, she would focus on the one thing she could do.

"Tell me about your relationship with Geffin Chardan."

"Geffin Chardan?" Chikkit blinked a few times, her ears twitching. "I don't have a relationship with him. I've only met him one time!"

"Many ministers on Thlist know him. Tell me everything."

"Oh. Of course." With a glance at Joranran, Chikkit sat behind her desk. "He's from here. Well, he grew up here, went to the same school as many of my colleagues. They're all from the same clique." Distaste colored her tone, and she didn't act like she wanted to hide it. "He's a horrible man, Officer. He has dirt on everyone. The longer he knows them, the more he can hold over them. Why do you think he serves such short prison terms? Someone always arranges to give him early release. If he doesn't escape, that is."

The files Vilstair had on Chardan didn't mention him living on Thlist. The files had little about his childhood. She hadn't bothered digging deeper, only taking what she had. When she tapped her jewel to search for more information, it appeared before her eyes: his school reports, all of which came from Thlist. She also found mention of various parole boards granting him early release from prison.

"Do any of the ministers here have a connection to his gang?"

Chikkit shrugged. "I don't discuss Chardan with my colleagues, Officer. Like I said, I met him once, a few years ago. I didn't care for him. The only reason I know this much is because of the favor he called us about a day ago."

Vilstair leaned forward. Finally, a useful clue. "Tell me about it."

"I can show you." Chikkit tapped her jewel.

Images appeared on the left wall of her office, showing a ship's bridge. It was a medium-sized bridge, appropriate for a frigate-class ship, the same type as the *Otteran*. Chardan sat in the captain's chair, a number of his crew members at nearby stations. Vilstair didn't see Farovan, though she looked.

"My crew and I will be visiting Thlist tomorrow," Chardan said in the recording.

"Oh?" said a man's voice from off-screen. The Prime Minister of Thlist, according to the text at the bottom of the image. "What do you need to hide from this time, Geffin? It's hard enough to hide you from the Neutrals. Are you still planning to go against the Gray? Only crazy people do that, you know."

Chardan waved a hand. "I know what I'm doing. It will be worth it, I promise. Are you familiar with the actor Koryan Jorn, better known as Koyanran Joranran?"

"Of course," the Prime Minister said. "Everyone knows him."

"He's a horrible man." Chardan leaned forward, lacing his fingers together. Beside Vilstair, Joranran made a soft sound. "He is personally financing the horrors being conducted on Ill-gottens by the Hreckin government."

"What do you mean? I know that planet's anti-Ill-gotten, but horrors?"

"They've been keeping it quiet. They have to, if they want to keep their Neutral status. They're trying to develop a virus, Prime Minister, one that only affects people with mixed DNA. The virus will break apart those mixed bonds, killing the person. They're close to finishing this virus. Very close."

"That's not true," Joranran said, but his voice was weak.

Vilstair wrapped her arms around herself. A virus that only killed Ill-gottens? And only a few generations after they had become stable and viable? Monstrous indeed. The Gray would never stand for such a thing. Neither would the Light or the Neutral. The Dark would probably love it, but most of the galactic senate ignored the Dark.

After a silence, the Prime Minister said, "Do you want us

to report this to the senate? It would be better coming from an operative. They would ask how we came to learn about it. Thlist has no particular ties with Hreckin."

Chardan shook his head. "Thank you, but no. We'll take care of the political side. There's another reason I'm asking. In a few hours, my crew and I will come to Thlist. We'll be chased by Joranran and a Gray operative. An Ill-gotten Gray operative. We need you to secure those two. They need to be safe when the senate comes to ask questions."

Murmuring came from the recording — not from the *Otteran*'s bridge, but from the other side. "From what you said about Joranran, we would have cause to hold him for a time," the Prime Minister said, causing the murmurs to quiet. "But you want us to detain a Gray operative? Are you insane?"

"Think of it as protective custody. She will need your help, Prime Minister. After all, she'll already be in Joranran's company. If we leave her there for long, she'll be killed."

Though she knew he was harmless — discounting his asshole-ish tendencies — Vilstair shifted her chair away from Joranran, moving so that she could keep an eye on him. Her hands clenched on the sides of the chair.

"Very well," the Prime Minister said. "But no harm will come to the operative."

"I should hope not. She's the key to all of this. Thank you for your help. I'll see you soon. *Otteran* out." The call and the recording ended.

When Joranran shifted in his chair, Vilstair pointed her blaster at him. "Don't move!"

"Vilstair! You can't believe that I'd hurt you, can you? I told you that I love you now!" He looked even more pathetic than he had earlier.

"This virus. Is it real? Do you have any with you?"

"Yes, but I would never use it."

Her hand trembled before she forced it steady. "Show me. Slowly."

Joranran reached inside his jacket. His movements were so slow that Vilstair nearly told him to hurry up. Chikkit watched in silence, her ears quivering. After a brief rummage, Joranran produced a small box, which he held out for her.

According to her jewel, there were four pills inside. Did the virus have to be ingested for it to work? Vilstair shoved the box into one of her jacket's inner pockets. It was a sturdy thing that wouldn't easily break. Still, the first chance she got, she'd stow it safely on the *Nebula's Edge*.

She tapped her jewel, trying to get hold of Shinead again. Nothing. No Butler or strike team either. Then she tried back home.

Yafan's image appeared before her eyes. "Vilstair! You escaped!" He sat up straight, looking less tired than he had a moment ago.

"I can't get ahold of Shinead or the Gray strike team. What's going on?"

"I don't know. I can't reach anyone either." Yafan shook his head, his ears flapping with the movement. "The strike team should be there. We received notification when they dropped out of hyperspace, a few minutes ago."

Vilstair frowned. "Farovan has done something. I know it." She gave Yafan a quick summary of what had happened: her escape, the details about Chardan and his connections here, and, most importantly, the four pills Joranran gave her. She held out the box with the pills, though Yafan wouldn't be able to get a reading on it from Diresi. Throughout her report, Yafan bared his teeth more and more.

After a glance to the side, Yafan said, "We finally got a reading on the strike team's ship. It's in orbit around Thlist, near the edge of the system and coming no closer. We've been hailing them, but they won't respond. We've sent out another team."

Vilstair crossed her arms over her chest, trying to make it look casual instead of the need for comfort. "Is that wise? Farovan will attack them too."

"You need to do something about Farovan before he messes with everyone's minds. The next strike team will include saireishi. Vilstair, do you remember how to defend yourself against a saireishi?"

She swallowed. It had been part of her training, but she'd never had to practice it. Most operatives never met saireishi, thank the Gray gods. Even on her recent trip to Rolleron and working past the drugged up, Unattached saireishi, she hadn't used it. Those saireishi had only been trying to distract her. They hadn't attacked her mind directly.

"I know what to do," she said because there wasn't anything else to say.

"Keep me apprised every hour. Change jewels if you need to. Be careful, and may the Gray gods watch over you." Yafan hung up.

It wasn't what she hoped. She had hoped the problem was a minor communication one, something with her jewel or with Shinead's jewel. She had hoped that Shinead and the strike team were fine and had already defeated Farovan, Chardan, and the others. She didn't want to meet Farovan again. Just being on the same planet as him made her want to flee.

She was a Gray operative, and she was the only one who could help. The strike team's ship hadn't been blown up. Gray gods willing, they were all still alive and waiting to be rescued. Shinead and Butler too. The next strike team wouldn't arrive for hours. That might be too late. The only person who could help was Vilstair, much as she didn't want to.

She recalled everything that Farovan and Chardan had

done, all their pitiful justifications. Even the virus that killed only Ill-gotten didn't change anything. They could have found that and reported it to the Gray or the senate without killing anyone. And how did the theft enter into this?

A chill ran down her spine, and she turned to Joranran. He had been slumped over in his chair. When she looked at him, he perked up. "What did the thieves steal?" Vilstair asked.

"We gave you a list, didn't we?"

"There was something of yours that they took. You never said."

Joranran hunched his shoulders. "You don't want to know. It was from before I fell in love with you."

"They stole the virus, didn't they." She knew it with sudden clarity.

Joranran winced and ducked his head. "Yes. Almost all the copies."

The *Otteran* took more than just the virus. For some reason, Farovan didn't want to go public about the virus yet. So he stole other items too, to hide the fact that he took the virus. Soon, he would tell the galaxy about that. He wanted to take down everyone on Hreckin, so that had to be part of his plan.

Vilstair wasn't good at planning. There was a reason she was a law enforcement operative and not part of the military. Whatever plan Farovan had concocted, she couldn't guess. If she could find him and stop him, she didn't need to know.

She still had her jewel and the one she took from Drinfer. Chardan and Farovan were on both contact lists. Vilstair started searching.

Both thieves were together, in a building a mile away. From here, Vilstair couldn't determine any details. She didn't need to. She knew her duty.

"Thank you for your help," she told Chikkit. "Please

keep in regular contact with Diresi, even if you learn nothing new."

The Huckfering nodded, looking frightened. Vilstair wondered if Farovan would come after Chikkit. She wondered too if he already had. If Chikkit did something to betray her, there was nothing she could do about it. She had to focus on Farovan.

Head held hide in an attempt to contain her fear, Vilstair left the office.

14

The first report on Hreckin came shortly after Madrigan took care of the Gray strike team. He tapped his jewel, making the report appear on the far wall of the room, where everyone could see it. In the report, newsreader stood with images of Hreckin projected behind him.

"A Gray investigation team on Hreckin has discovered that, as actor Koryan Jorn, better known as Koyanran Joranran, claimed, the Natural Birth Order has offices on the Neutral planet, which were sponsored by the government. For over one hundred and fifty years, Ill-gotten children were taken to Hreckin or bred in captivity, where they were then experimented on until they died." The reporter said everything with an equally bland expression and tone.

Madrigan glared at the man. Most reporters showed little emotion, especially ones from Capitania. Capitania was the center of the galaxy, where the Unattached lived and where the senate convened. Most people there at least pretended to not have biases.

If there was anything that should cause a reaction in any sentient being — except maybe a Dark path — it was hearing about experimentation on children. Perhaps the reporter was Dark path. Perhaps he was so inured to reporting that he didn't emote when he spoke.

At the moment, Madrigan didn't care. He hated the reporter.

"The Gray has introduced a motion to the senate," the reporter continued, voice still bland. "It will determine the fate of Hreckin and its citizens. The senate has begun debates on the motion." He then switched to talking about trade tariffs, at which point his voice gained animation.

Disgusted with him and with the galaxy in general, Madrigan turned off the feed.

"We should have just attacked Hreckin directly," Polf said. "The senate takes forever to decide anything, and they rarely agree."

"What will happen to Hreckin?" Loddrin asked. "Will the senate condemn them?"

Polf waved a pincer. "The whole senate probably won't. I bet you one hundred credits that the Dark offers Hreckin sanctuary or alliance."

"No bet." Loddrin pulled a face. "I'm not that dumb."

With a groan, Madrigan turned away from them. He and Geffin had debated this part of the plan for a long time. Once the truth about Hreckin came out, its fate was no longer in their hands. Madrigan wished that the Light had been the ones to investigate Hreckin first, not the Gray. The Light was firm on its opinions about child abuse. They would have killed everyone on Hreckin without bothering to ask the senate about its opinion.

Since Hreckin was still newly Neutral, the Light could only investigate if called there. They had no territory near Hreckin, and thus no excuse to be in the area. The Light had never been a real possibility, only the Neutral and the Gray.

Only if all four alignments — Light, Gray, Neutral, and Dark — voted Hreckin out of the senate would the entire planet suffer. That was fine with Madrigan. All four alignments rarely agreed, but they didn't need to.

Hreckin would be without nearby allies, without allies who could protect them. The Dark would probably offer an alliance in exchange for the virus. No one on Hreckin had access to the virus anymore — Madrigan made sure of that. Without that, they had no negotiating power, and the Dark wouldn't long be interested in them.

The Neutral liked to stand aside, and the Gray preferred to settle matters like this within the confines of the senate. The Light had opinions on child abuse, though, very strong opinions. Hreckin would soon be without allies, without a place in the galaxy. If the Light declared war on Hreckin, no one would stop them.

Madrigan fancied the idea of Hreckin being ruined by the Light. He was a good guy now, and so the Light should be on his side.

The Light wouldn't torture or capture anyone on Hreckin — they didn't do things like that. They would be willing to kill everyone on the planet if they thought everyone was involved. Though not everyone on Hreckin had been involved in the experiments, they were all there because they shared a hatred for Ill-gotten. That would hopefully be enough for the Light to declare Hreckin anathema.

Even if the Light didn't wage war against Hreckin, the people there could no longer continue as they had been. They would be without trading partners, without any rights in the galaxy. As such, they couldn't stay on Hreckin. No other planet would want a refuge from Hreckin, too afraid of being similarly estranged.

It wasn't a grandiose end, but it was an end nonetheless. Madrigan thought he liked it all the better for being so pathetic. It was only what the people of Hreckin deserved.

The door slammed open, and Geffin and two other crew members came inside. They had left a few minutes ago to speak with some Thlist officials. "Officer Bila has escaped," Geffin said, fury painted across his face.

Madrigan blinked and reached out. He found the cell

where he'd left Vilstair. There was a Human male nearby, unconscious, but he found no sign of Vilstair. She had indeed escaped.

He'd been distracted while hunting for the Gray strike team. With his attention so dispersed, he hadn't been able to keep track of anything else.

"Should I look for her?" he asked. She would be hard to find, her mind so slippery. If he concentrated long and hard, he would find her, no matter where on Thlist she tried to hide.

"Another Gray strike team will be coming soon. We can't afford to have you distracted." Geffin stared at Madrigan as he spoke.

Madrigan huffed. "I'm fine, Geffin, I told you. Putting twenty people to sleep isn't hard."

"There isn't anything Bila can do against us. Not now. Leave her be. You need to watch for the next strike team." Geffin began to pace as he spoke, the anger on his face turned to worry.

He didn't like it when plans went awry. That was why he and Madrigan spent so much time planning this. It occurred to Madrigan suddenly that they hadn't spoken about what would happen to Hreckin, now that the entire galaxy knew about its crimes and now that Geffin could no longer control events.

"Let me look for her, Geffin," he said. "It won't take long, I promise. Another strike team must still be hours away."

This was his first plan, but Madrigan decided he also didn't like it when things went against how they should go. However cruel Vilstair was, she wasn't incompetent, and she wasn't a fool. It was dangerous to leave her out where she could cause any amount of trouble.

"You leave Vilstair alone!"

The feminine voice behind him made Madrigan blink. He

turned to see their prisoners both awake. Shinead glared at him, wiggling in an attempt to escape her restraints. Butler was calmer but no less unhappy.

Madrigan checked the time. They had been out for a few hours, so they'd been due to wake up soon. Actually, they should have woken earlier. Maybe they'd been faking sleep. He hadn't thought to check since they couldn't do anything to stop him.

Loddrin marched over to the two captives, waving his blaster in their faces. "You wanna get shot again? No? Then shut the fuck up!"

"If you think you can attack me or Vilstair, you don't know much about the Gray!" Shinead didn't look afraid of the blaster. "We will find you, and we will stop you. No one escapes Gray justice."

"Yeah, but you won't be worried about it." With a nasty grin, Loddrin switched his blaster from stun to kill mode.

Polf strode over to him and slapped his hand down. That made Loddrin's blaster point at the floor. He hadn't had his finger on the trigger, but Madrigan relaxed anyway.

"Stop that," Polf said. "You trying to be a criminal again? We're the good guys, remember? The Gray will come around, but not if you threaten their operatives."

"Sorry." Loddrin ducked his head and put his blaster back on stun mode. "Doesn't mean we have to listen to them."

"If they talk again, stun them," Geffin said. "Otherwise, I'd rather leave them alone. Madrigan, don't bother with Bila. I'm sure she'll try something, but it doesn't matter now. The galaxy knows about what Hreckin did. The senate will soon decide their fate. The Gray might harass us, but it doesn't matter if they stop us now. Nothing can save Hreckin, and that's what matters."

Madrigan hunched his shoulders and wondered.

Hreckin was already doomed, that was true. But would the Gray stop their pursuit of himself and the rest of the *Otteran* crew? If Vilstair was like most of the Gray, and he thought she was, they would rather imprison everyone. The Gray loved to arrest people, no matter how minor or justified their crime.

He couldn't allow that. If Geffin was captured again, he'd spend the rest of his life deep in a Gray prison. Geffin didn't talk much about it, but Madrigan knew he feared that above all else. Polf, Loddrin, Bakigan, and some of the others would face a similar fate. Perhaps they all would, even those with shorter and less severe criminal records.

Only Madrigan would avoid that fate. The Gray would try to recruit him. Saireishi were rare, and one as powerful as he would be wasted in prison. Once the Gray learned they couldn't win or buy his loyalty, they would probably kill him. They couldn't afford to have him running around loose.

If he got captured by the Gray, so be it. Now that they knew about him, they would never stop pursuing him. He had been prepared for that since he and Geffin conceived this plan. But he would not let the Gray have Geffin and the others.

He was here to protect his friends. They were only here because of him. Though Madrigan loved them all, he knew what sort of people they were. He didn't need experience with people or to look into their minds. The crew of the *Otteran* was scum, the dregs of society. They didn't care about a few dozen Ill-gotten children who had suffered on Hreckin, especially as most of those children were already dead.

No, they cared a little, but not enough to risk their lives and future freedom for it. Thanks to Geffin, the entire crew was rich. They could have all left after arriving on Thlist, as most of them had. The ones that remained were Madrigan's friends.

He knew little about friendship, but he knew this. He had to protect them, no matter what the cost to himself. They were here for him, and so he would make sure they left Thlist alive and free.

Vilstair was out there, already causing trouble. Madrigan didn't know what she might plan. Without lots of time and effort, he couldn't find her.

Neither could he predict when the next Gray strike team might arrive. They would be more formidable than the last, possibly enough to defeat him. Madrigan knew himself to be powerful, but his childhood taught him that power and skill weren't always enough.

It was luck that saved him on Hreckin. He didn't give the gods credit for it. He knew that the gods didn't care about his life. Any child might have been the one to survive the laboratory exploding — if the gods had been kind, perhaps many children could have survived. Equally, no one might have lived. If anyone should have lived, it was the youngest child, the most powerful one, the one whose talents Madrigan spurred into early existence.

Instead, Madrigan lived. He valued his life and freedom, and he wanted vengeance for those who hadn't made it. He now wanted a life for his friends. It was what the other children would have wanted, he thought, if they could have cared for one another.

He was saireishi. He could pluck thoughts from another being's mind, change their personality, and track anyone down. He was not a god. There were plenty of powers he didn't have. He wasn't parreishi, granted with the power of his patron god. He wasn't kireishi, able to empower his body and perform amazing physical feats. He wasn't reishi, but then no one was.

He couldn't predict the future. Some priests of Fate could, or so people said. Madrigan had never met a Fate priest, let alone a Fate priest with parreishi. Even they couldn't determine how things might end on Thlist, he thought.

Since he didn't know and couldn't learn, he should make some contingencies. With Vilstair and the next strike team nowhere to be found, he had nothing else to do.

Geffin might call him a fool and scold him. Madrigan didn't care. He would save Geffin and the others, no matter what.

He let his eyes droop to half-mast as he stretched out his mind. Since he didn't know what the future held, he could only make so many plans. He could, however, control the mind of any person in this building.

Since leaving Hreckin, he'd never used his full powers. Perhaps it was time he did so.

15

Before she left the building, Vilstair noticed the person shadowing her. They were good, but she'd been followed before. She continued at the same pace, forcing her body to stay loose and calm.

Outside the building at the corner, she caught a bus which would take her south, towards Farovan and Chardan. She sat at the front of the bus, angled sideways so she could see the other passengers. Just before the doors closed, a person slipped on and took a seat near the back. He had a hood pulled up, but Vilstair knew who he was. Joranran hadn't bothered to change his clothes.

Of course, it would be too easy to just leave him behind. She hadn't told him he could come with, but when did he listen? Now that he thought he loved her, he was even more annoying.

When he caught her staring at him, he grinned and waved. Vilstair groaned as he stood and joined her at the front. "You noticed me."

"Of course I noticed you." He'd done a good job at following her. She didn't say that since she didn't want to encourage him.

"I learned how to follow people during some of my holocins." Vilstair only rolled her eyes a little. Joranran leaned closer. "Why did you leave me behind, Vilstair? I want to help you. After everything I've done, you must give me a chance to make up for it."

"No, I really don't have to." Getting rid of him might cause more of a disturbance than bringing him along. Farovan must know that she'd escaped. He'd be looking for her. She could defend herself a little from a saireishi, but only if he wasn't aware of her. If he was waiting for her, actively searching for her, she would never take him by surprise.

"Vilstair, please." He reached for her hands.

She twisted and shoved her hands under her armpits, out of reach. "You want to be helpful?" He nodded. "Fine. But you have to do exactly as I say." She was fighting a saireishi. A distraction would be wonderful.

"I will do whatever you tell me to do." He was far too earnest.

Though he leaned in close, clearly waiting for details, Vilstair refused to say anything else. A mile south of where they caught it, they got off the bus, a block from the building where Farovan and Chardan were. Vilstair kept her distance. She didn't know Farovan's range. The most powerful of saireishi could detect thoughts from this distance, but only if they had a visual or a close connection. Or at least knew to search for a person. Vilstair kept to the side of the street, avoiding security cameras.

She circled the building from a block away, studying it. Her jewel scanned the interior, forming a map for her. Farovan and Chardan were on the twelfth floor with thirty other people. Crew members from the *Otteran*, but there might be locals among them, possibly including officials. Drinfer's jewel didn't recognize the other people, and he should know all the officials, so she hoped not.

"They're on the twelfth floor," she told Joranran. "Can you distract them for me?"

He puffed out his chest. "Of course I can. Can I make it public?" He grinned evilly, clearly plotting something.

She didn't trust him or like him, but with his brain scrambled, he was on her side. So long as it kept attention away from her, she shouldn't complain. "Have fun."

"Great." He rubbed his hands together. "Give me an hour. I need to prepare." He leaned in for a hug. Vilstair forced herself to stand still and accept it. When he pulled closer for a kiss, that was too much. Vilstair slipped out of his embrace and away. Though he pouted for a moment, he grinned at her one last time before heading off.

Farovan could hack his brain again, Vilstair thought as she watched him leave. Even if Joranran was on her side now, he might not stay there. So long as he stayed on her side for the next hour or so, that was all she needed.

She had more important things to do than worry. An hour wasn't long to get into position. She couldn't move yet, not without her mental defenses in place.

Vilstair made a mental list of some of the most annoying songs she knew. It would be a miserable hour, but she had been trained to handle pain. She picked one of the less stupid ones and tapped Drinfer's jewel. The song began playing, loud enough for people nearby to hear. Most of them made disgusted faces, and one man yelled at Vilstair to keep her rubbish music to herself. One teenage girl — and if there was any subset of the population who displayed no taste, it was teenagers — started dancing and singing along. The man who had shouted looked ill as he quickly walked away.

As she walked closer to the building, Vilstair sang softly. Sadly, she knew the lyrics to the song. It was played all the time because people had no concept of good music. Though a number of other people grumbled at her, Vilstair didn't switch the audio to reach only her ears.

She concentrated hard on the lyrics and how she sang them, letting everything else slip from her mind. She wanted to cringe, to stop, but she kept going. By the time she reached the building, she'd gone through two songs and had started a third, this one far worse than the other two. Even the teenagers glared at her for that song.

The atrium of the building was open to the public. Most of it belonged to various businesses. Vilstair had her jewel record the list, but she couldn't think about it. Not when all her concentration remained on the bad songs. She only noted that the twelfth floor housed a shipping company.

She didn't head upstairs. Instead she found the security office on the first floor. A tap of her jewel flashed her identification, and the door opened for her.

An overweight Human sat inside, three robots watching the monitors. "Officer, what in the hells are you listening to?"

"I need this music." It was hard to talk and focus on the music at the same time. She had rehearsed these words, which helped. She couldn't afford to stop listening to the music, not with Farovan just a few floors above her. "You need to play this list of music throughout the building for the next standard hour."

"Please tell me you're kidding." He looked ill.

"This is an official Gray operation. I require your assistance." Sweat beaded her brow. She couldn't argue with him for long.

With a sigh that suggested great suffering and sacrifice, the guard tapped his jewel, copying the list of music from her. Then he transferred the list to the speakers throughout the building and locked the list into place.

As soon as he dropped his hand from his jewel, Vilstair stunned him. He twitched and fell to the ground, hitting hard. "At least you won't have to hear any of this," Vilstair told him. While he was unconscious, Farovan couldn't do anything to him. She didn't like to stun civilians, but she had no choice. She took his jewel, just in case.

Locking the door to the security office behind her,

Vilstair silenced the music from her jewel. She didn't need that now, not with the music pipping through the building. Most buildings had speakers placed throughout them in case people needed to be warned about emergencies and didn't have their jewels. It was standard practice on Gray and Neutral worlds. Even a saireishi like Farovan shouldn't be able to turn the music off remotely. Only someone with access to the security office could do that, and the guard wouldn't do anything for a few hours.

She hummed along as she took the stairs up. With Farovan nearby, she didn't want to risk the lift. At each landing, she paused to check the layout of the floors. With the stupid music commanding most of her attention, she could only notice cursory details. No one had stopped the music, so her plan hadn't gone wrong yet.

When she reached the eleventh floor, she stopped. She hunkered down in the stairwell, her jewel scanning the next floor in detail. She sang more loudly, listening intently to the lyrics. Gray gods, she hated this song. She heard it on Rolleron while chasing down Globlan. This song played over the speakers while she searched for the drugged up saireishi.

This song might have saved her then. It might have distracted the saireishi, so that they could only throw illusions at her.

It might have saved her life, but she still hated it. Her hand clenched on her blaster, and she kept singing.

Farovan and Chardan were still in the same room as earlier. Now only twenty people waited with them, instead of thirty. Vilstair had hoped the music might have dragged a few more people away, but ten was better than none. Her jewel informed her that the speakers in that room had been disabled — smashed and beyond easy repair. She hoped Farovan hated this music even more than she did.

With a wince, Vilstair pushed that thought from her

mind and paid attention only to the lyrics. Farovan would be more sensitive to thoughts against him. She couldn't slip up now, not when she was so close.

Twenty more minutes before Joranran's hour elapsed. Assuming he could accurately estimate the amount of time he needed. That thought was far too deliberate, so Vilstair couldn't brood over it. She slowly headed to the twelfth floor.

There was no one out front of the staircase — her jewel told her that. Her paranoia demanded that she crouch down and keep close to the wall, blaster drawn and ready. She no longer sung, but continued to hum. It gave her something to focus on besides her worry. For that, she could almost appreciate the annoying but distracting song. Other than the twenty people in the room with Farovan and Chardan, she saw two others near the lift and one in a room on the opposite side of the building. Shinead and Butler might be with Farovan, along with local officials.

Vilstair shook her head. She wasn't supposed to be thinking this hard. Farovan had to be listening. Vilstair let her head loll back to rest against the wall. She closed her eyes and heard the lyrics. She let the lyrics consume her, no longer even cringing at how banal they were.

When only the lyrics remained in her mind, she moved away from the stairs. There was a room adjacent to the one where Farovan and Chardan were. Whatever Joranran had planned, it would help if Vilstair was close. She took a circuitous route to the adjacent room, making sure she went nowhere near the lift.

The door to this room stood on a different hallway. Vilstair kept her back to the wall as she walked along, ready to move if anyone came into view. The music was softer here since the speaker at the intersection had been shot. It was loud enough. When she reached the door, she groped the knob blindly, her back to the door. It turned under her hand.

Vilstair dove through the door, whirling around and bringing up her blaster.

The lights flickered on at her entrance, showing an empty room filled with boxes. Vilstair let out a long breath, then began to hum again. She closed and locked the door behind her, checking every side to be sure she was alone. It wasn't other people she worried about — her jewel confirmed no other life signs — but recording equipment. Other than the security camera near the ceiling, she found nothing. The guard and robots downstairs should have been the only ones with access to the feed from that camera, but she couldn't risk it. 'Sorry,' she mouthed, then shot the camera.

The wall on the left joined the room with Farovan, Chardan, and the others. A check with her jewel still showed twenty people inside. Vilstair tapped her jewel a few times, but she couldn't get a feed on that room. The thieves must have broken the security camera in there, just like she had in here.

She had expected that. There was an air duct which connected every room on the floor. Still humming, Vilstair detached the cover, then reached into her jacket pocket. She took out the camera and switched it on. It should be safe — saireishi read people, not technology. After tapping her jewel to ensure the connection, she tossed the camera into the air ducts.

It hovered along slowly so that it didn't collide with the walls. When it reached the next vent, Vilstair had it stop. She smiled as images appeared on the wall before her, joined a moment later by sound. Now she could see and hear everything that happened next door. She could record it all with her jewel since she couldn't concentrate on it too much, lest Farovan notice her.

Even knowing that, she still nearly gave herself away when she noticed some of the other people in the room.

Shinead and Butler were there, manacled to chairs on the side of the room, bruised, bloodied, unarmed, and clearly angry, but otherwise fine. Shinead had twisted in her chair, her fingers busy with the manacles that held her in place. Vilstair didn't think Shinead could wiggle free, but she offered her partner a silent cheer anyway.

The others in the room paid the prisoners little attention, absorbed instead on the image that showed on the wall. The background showed the senate building on Capitania, a sight every civilized being in the galaxy recognized. A Ditilish woman stood out front, reporting on the day's news.

"—and the world Fitervan has been confirmed as Neutral," the woman said. She paused to tap her jewel, her antennae twitching. "The senate has just begun discussing the reports from the Neutral world Hreckin. Investigators report that Hreckin has developed chemical weapons that would target Ill-gotten beings, killing them in a matter of minutes. The Light and Gray sections of the senate have moved for the virus to be classified as a weapon of mass destruction. The Gray and the Neutral want a thorough investigation into everyone involved in the development of the virus so that those beings can be arrested. The Light has moved that all of Hreckin should be placed under arrest, and the Dark has offered all sentients from Hreckin amnesty inside their territory. We will update you as the discussion continues."

"That's it?" Chardan sounded disgusted as he lowered the volume. "They should be taking ministers and scientists into custody already!"

Farovan shook his head. "It's the galactic senate. Nothing happens fast there."

"What if they don't do anything? How much of a majority do they need to get everyone on Hreckin?" Chardan waved his hands as he spoke.

After tapping his jewel, Farovan sighed. "The senate

would require that Light, Gray, Neutral, and Dark all vote against Hreckin before the entire population could be arrested — and we all know that will never happen. The Dark has probably already offered a fortune for the virus."

"Will they get it?"

"Of course not! The Light and Gray and Neutral would never allow that! Honestly, Chardan, you're taking the Dark too seriously! They used to be dangerous, but these days they attack themselves and only threaten the rest of the universe. They—" Farovan's brow furrowed.

Quickly, Vilstair started singing again. He mustn't hear her thoughts. He couldn't even know that she was nearby.

"Stop that," Farovan said, turning on Shinead. When she glared, he sighed and took out his blaster. Vilstair stiffened against her will, but Farovan only stunned Shinead.

"I thought you wanted witnesses to this farce of yours," Butler said. Farovan turned to him, and Vilstair silently blessed the man. Hopefully, he would help distract Farovan for her. At least until she got her anger under control.

"We have all the witnesses we need." Chardan watched Farovan, clearly concerned. The saireishi had turned to the side, massaging his temples and muttering under his breath.

There were a number of ways to stop a saireishi. The best method involved avoiding their attention — Vilstair couldn't do that. Not just because she was Ill-gotten and thus of interest to Farovan. As a Gray officer, she was bound to stop him.

The next best method was the one she employed: thinking distracting thoughts so that the saireishi couldn't pick up anything useful. It had shortcomings. For one, she had to keep singing the damn songs. For another, if Farovan actually concentrated on her, he would still be able to get inside her head.

The last method was the best. If many people thought

loud things at the same time, a saireishi could be overwhelmed. With only herself and Joranran, Vilstair hadn't considered that method. It seemed there might be truth to it, given the way Farovan acted. If he kept stunning people, they wouldn't be able to use it.

She hoped Butler was having lots of loud and sadistic thoughts. That should keep Farovan from noticing her. If those thoughts annoyed the saireishi, all the better.

Chardan walked over to Farovan and put a hand on his shoulder. "You're getting tense. Taking out that strike team was too much. You should rest. Me and the boys can finish taking care of this." Some of the others in the room.

"No, I'm fine. I just need—" Farovan straightened suddenly, staring at the wall which such intensity, it was as if he could see through it. He might be able to see through it. "Someone's nearby."

Vilstair sang harder, clutching her blaster close. She could sing and defend herself at the same time if she needed to. How she would defeat twenty people by herself, she didn't know.

"Who? Where?" Chardan tapped his jewel and drew his own weapon.

Farovan stared in the opposite direction from Vilstair. After a moment, a look of disgust crossed his face. "Gods. It's Jorn."

"What? Why?" Chardan lowered his blaster.

"I don't know." When Chardan raised an eyebrow, Farovan shook his head. "He's singing along with that damn song. Why in the hells is it still playing through the rest of the building? I can't concentrate!"

"Hey, calm down. We're working on the song. As for Jorn, let him come. He can't do anything to us. You've already captured his mind."

That seemed to make Farovan feel better — the tension

between his shoulders eased. "That's true. Let him in so we can make him stop singing," he told one of the others.

The man left the room and returned a few seconds later with Joranran. The man kept a tight grip on the actor though Joranran made no attempt at escape. He sang the song, though it couldn't be heard in the room, perfectly in tune of course, the bastard.

"Stop that," Chardan said. Joranran kept on singing.

"Stop," Farovan said, a crease between his brows. Joranran shut up. "Thank you. Now, what's the problem? You're supposed to be with Vilstair."

She wouldn't have much time. Perhaps Joranran's distraction hadn't unfolded as he wished. Perhaps this was all he had planned. Perhaps none of it mattered against a saireishi. However minor this distraction was, it might be the best Vilstair would get. She wanted more, but she couldn't wait.

The camera in the vent was connected to her jewel. That allowed her to see and hear what happened in the next room. The camera didn't just broadcast. It had all sorts of other features.

Vilstair tapped her jewel twice. The first closed down the ventilation between the rooms. That also stopped the feed, but she had no choice. The second tap released the gas.

Even before her finger left her jewel, Vilstair was up and moving. She hurried out of the room, blaster still clutched close and humming. She spotted no people outside the room where she'd hidden. Before she rounded the corner, her jewel picked up two people watching outside the room that held Farovan and the others. One man had turned around to face the door, working at the lock with a frantic expression. The other remained at guard.

By chance or perhaps a late but welcome blessing from the Gray gods, the other man was turned away when Vilstair rounded the corner. She didn't hesitate. She stunned him in the back. As he tipped over, she shot the other guard as he looked up. Both hit the ground hard. They'd be bruised from the wall and floor, but she felt no sympathy. They were part of the *Otteran* crew — she recognized them. They deserved this and far worse.

She paused to cuff both men's hands together and to one another, back to back to make it harder for them to escape. Then she sent a call to the local police to come. If she didn't survive — or if her mind didn't survive — perhaps someone else could stop Farovan.

The first guard hadn't opened the door. Vilstair lunged into it shoulder first, but it still didn't give. She scowled, backed off two steps, and switched her blaster to kill mode. When she shot this time, the red beam was brighter and wider than it usually was, the sizzling noise louder.

A hole burned through the lock. Ignoring the smoke issuing from the middle of the door, Vilstair threw herself against it again. With a creak, it bent then snapped open. She tumbled inside, falling to her knees as she raised her blaster, ready to be attacked.

Nothing moved inside the room. Smoke clung to the ceiling, slowly dissipating. When Vilstair tapped her jewel, the camera opened the vents. That and the open door got most of the gas out of the room. Even if it had lingered, it would have only made things harder to see. Knockout gas only affected people for the first few seconds after being de-pressurized. After that, it made Abernomes drowsy, but no other species suffered additional effects. There were no Abernomes in the *Otteran* crew, so Vilstair didn't have to worry.

Joranran lay near the door, while Chardan and Farovan sprawled in the center. Butler snored softly in his restraints, other crew members from the *Otteran* and minor officials scattered across the room.

Vilstair switched her blaster back to stun mode and worked her way through the room. She shot Farovan first, then Chardan, then each of the others in turn. She left Shinead and Butler alone. Though tempted to stun Joranran, she didn't. However much she disliked him, she knew how to be professional.

The camera floated out to rest in her hand. She turned it off and tucked it into a pocket. With nothing else to do, she then waited for the local police to arrive.

16

Madrigan regained consciousness but kept still. One of the many things he learned during his childhood was how to play at being asleep. If he was asleep, the scientists in the lab usually left him alone. He could stay still for hours if need be, while his mind roved about.

Quiet surrounded him. There were others nearby, but they were asleep or unconscious. Madrigan almost flinched and gave himself away when he found Geffin among them. Geffin was fine. Gassed and stunned, but fine. Madrigan had to fight down the sigh of relief as he checked the rest of the room.

It took him longer than it should have to identify Vilstair. There were other Ill-gottens on Thlist, but she should be familiar by now. Madrigan eased sideways into her mind and absorbed what had happened.

He had only been out for a few minutes. Vilstair had positioned herself nearby, close enough to listen in. She sang annoying songs to herself that echoed over the building's speaker. Madrigan had allowed himself to be distracted by the songs, and hadn't gone hunting for people singing along with them. Clearly, he should have.

Vilstair intended for Jorn to be a distraction. He hadn't done as good a job as she had wished, but he had been enough. Vilstair released a gas into the room that knocked everyone unconscious. When she arrived shortly after, she then stunned everyone but Shinead and Butler. Now Vilstair waited for the local authorities to arrive.

She had already contacted Diresi. They knew she had Madrigan and the others contained. The Gray strike team was on its way, would be here in less than an hour, and would contain multiple Gray saireishi. Madrigan was powerful, but many saireishi trained to work together to confine other saireishi? He didn't fancy those odds, not while still tired from the sleeping gas.

They'd been defeated. It was an ignoble defeat, something Geffin would rant over. He would rant less if he wasn't imprisoned.

Instead of searching for the next strike team — which, since they were still in hyperspace, would have been a waste of time — Madrigan had made contingencies. He was glad now that he had.

He reached out, beyond the room and beyond the building. He had to move slower than usual, the sleeping gas and the stun slowing his progress. A stun would have knocked anyone else out for an hour, at least. Among the many other experiments the scientists performed on him while he was growing up on Hreckin, Madrigan learned how to resist a stun. A stun only knocked him out for a minute. The sleeping gas accounted for the rest of the time he spent unconscious.

The local authorities gathered together a group of police across town, moving painfully slowly. The people in charge were friends of Geffin and in love with the money he gave them. They were in no rush. He had a few minutes yet.

The *Otteran* waited across town, where they left it. Bakigan sat in the pilot's chair, bored and unaware of the danger. Vilstair hadn't thought to stop him. That was good.

Before Vilstair arrived, Madrigan slipped a few commands into Bakigan's mind. They were nothing that would hurt him: Madrigan liked him less than Geffin and Polf, but he still considered Bakigan a friend. So long as he didn't activate the commands, Bakigan would never know they were there.

It only took one quick prod.

Bakigan jerked up in his seat, blinking a few times. A distress signal flashed across his eyes. He thought it came via his jewel. Instead, it came directly from his brain, but he didn't need to know that. The distress call told him where to go and to go quickly.

He lunged for the controls as the *Otteran*'s engines hummed to life.

It should take less than a minute for him to arrive. The *Otteran* was far too large to land on the roof of this building. It could hover alongside it, but nothing more. Neither could it reach the twelfth story, where Madrigan's friends currently lay unconscious.

Madrigan shifted his attention closer, back inside the building. He'd made multiple contingencies for a reason.

In the security office on the first floor, the guard sprawled on the floor stunned into unconsciousness. Madrigan had placed a command into his mind less than an hour ago — Vilstair must have found him in the interim. No matter. The guard was already beginning to stir into wakefulness.

Madrigan slipped deeper into the guard's mind, letting the waves nearly overwhelm him. When he was as deep as he dared, he sent out a shock. It flashed through the waves, shoving them in the opposite direction.

The guard woke with a curse, nearly slamming his head into one of the nearby consoles. He blinked, trying to figure out what had happened. The terrible music, which still filled his office and most of the rest of the building, made it harder.

Madrigan gave him no chance to escape his control. He

found the command he left behind and pushed on it.

The guard hit a quick series of buttons, his gaze barely focusing. When he finished, he groaned and slumped over, passing out again.

Robots filled the building — Madrigan had the guard send them out earlier. People needed any amount of assistance, any number of errands run. Thus, most large business buildings kept a supply of robots on hand. If anyone else in this building needed a robot over the last hour, they were out of luck. All the robots were on the twelfth floor, a few doors down, waiting for the guard to issue this command.

They left the storage room where they'd been waiting, traveling in a quick line down the hall. The door to this room hung off its hinges, where Vilstair had broken it.

She heard their approach and turned to see what the commotion was, raising her blaster. A blaster on stun would put a robot out of commission until it could be restarted. Madrigan didn't have the time to waste on that, not with the *Otteran* already on its way, the local police and the Gray strike team not far behind. These robots didn't have blasters, not even ones that could only stun. They had no defense against Vilstair.

Madrigan tried to move. His body ached. Though he could fend off the mental effects of a stun, his body was slow and clumsy. Vilstair shifted to the side so that she could still look towards the door while also watching him. He wouldn't be able to take her by force.

With a grunt of effort that he normally wouldn't require, Madrigan flung himself into her mind. He fumbled and nearly missed. Maybe with practice, one day she wouldn't be hard to reach, but for now, he struggled.

"Get out." Vilstair's voice wavered — she must have realized what he was doing. She tried to sing along with the song. Though it had been shut off in this room, it played loudly from out in the hallway. Madrigan wished he could have made the guard downstairs turn it off. He hadn't placed that command in the guard in advance, and he was too tired for it now.

"Stay there." He couldn't put her to sleep, not with her wary against him and with him so weak. Her finger was already on the trigger of her blaster, and Madrigan had to fight to keep it from moving.

The muscles in Vilstair's body strained as she fought his control, and the waves of her mind rose up against him. "I won't let you escape. I know you have the virus."

"Virus?"

The robots were inside the room with them. They headed over without hesitation, ignoring Madrigan and Vilstair. There were eight robots, one for each member of the crew and one more besides. The robots were four feet high, cylindrical things that hovered an inch off the ground.

When they reached a crew member, arms shot out from the robots' sides. Those arms lifted the motionless crew members from the ground and draped them over top of the robot. It was an awkward position, and Madrigan hoped no one in the crew had back problems. Precarious too, though helped by the robots keeping one hand alongside for stability.

"The virus that is instantly deadly against all Ill-gotten." Sweat beaded Vilstair's face. Her blaster arm, now pointed at the empty door, trembled as she tried to force it back up. "You took it from the lab on Hreckin."

The last night in the laboratory on Hreckin, many things happened. It was luck and perhaps mercy from the gods that Madrigan had escaped.

The scientists put him to work. They wanted him to touch the mind of one of the children present, one too young to use sairei. There had never been a choice for Madrigan. He had to at least pretend to try. He slid into that terribly young mind. He planned to lie, to say that he tried but failed. He would be punished for it, but he didn't care. He wouldn't hurt a child.

Only one child at a time practiced sairei. The others would be kept in their cages, sedated. If some of the children worked together, they would be able to overwhelm the scientists.

In order to train and test the children, the scientists had to take the sedative away for short periods of time. That gave Madrigan and the children free rein with their power. He learned from an early age how to kill. It wasn't hard. Sink deep enough into a mind and pull in a specific way. People without the power of sairei had no defense against that.

The scientists knew that — in the early years of their experiments, many of them had died that way. Hence the development of the virus.

Canisters lined the sides of the training rooms and every cell, connected to the most refined sensors and fully automated. Even the scientists couldn't shut down the controls on the canisters. If the child being tested acted up in any way deemed inappropriate — which included trying to escape or trying to kill someone — the sensors triggered the canisters. The virus would flood the training room, airborne. The child would be dead in less than a minute.

Madrigan saw that happen to three other children at the laboratory. Though he often called himself a coward for it, he always obeyed the scientists. However terrible his life there was, he feared death more. So he obeyed, and so he lived.

That last day, he slipped into the mind of the young child. He triggered the child's sairei, at an age where the power was far too much. The child went mad. They lost control and struck out.

When the first scientist died from that onslaught, the

canisters triggered.

The canisters in the cells went off first. The ones in the training room where Madrigan was opened next. He would have died too except for the scientist in the room with him. The scientists at the laboratory had no fear of the virus: they weren't Ill-gotten.

It wasn't mercy or kindness from that scientist that saved Madrigan. It was luck or the gods or perhaps even the young child. The scientist had been standing by the door to the training room. When he died, he slumped over, which caused the door to open.

When the canisters opened with a hiss, Madrigan didn't hesitate. He ran out of the training room, kicking the dead scientist out of the way. He slammed the door shut behind him. There were no canisters in the hallway, and he breathed deep of clean air. If he had been a second or three slower, he would have died. The virus took less than a minute to kill.

He found himself alone in the corridors of the large complex, surrounded by the dead. He had never imagined freedom before that moment because that dream would have been too painful. He had it, though, suddenly and irrevocably. Perhaps he had never dreamed of that moment, much less planned it, but he didn't need to. He knew what to do.

The scientists had placed a second level of fail-safes throughout the laboratory. Unlike the canisters, these weren't automatic, but required one of the scientists to enter a code to activate them. They didn't tell the children about those codes, but Madrigan read everything from the scientists' minds years ago. He found a console, entered the code, and triggered the lab's self-destruct sequence. The scientists thought it was better to kill themselves and take down their experiment rather than let even one child escape.

On his run out of the laboratory, Madrigan spied an unopened canister. He paused to snatch it up, then ran faster. He barely made it out of the laboratory before it blew up. He didn't wait around for the Hreckin authorities to investigate. He didn't need to wait to know that no one else had survived.

Within hours, he stole a ship and left Hreckin, the canister still in his possession.

"Why would I want to kill Ill-gottens?" he asked Vilstair. He appeared Human unless a person looked very carefully at him. That had helped him escape Hreckin, had helped him blend into society until he met Geffin.

"You don't want any competition." Vilstair looked like she'd sprinted a marathon. If she kept straining so much, she'd hurt herself. Madrigan didn't have the strength to prevent her from that.

The last robot left the room, Polf hanging off of it. The *Otteran* should be seconds away. With no one conscious outside the room, Madrigan couldn't follow the course the robots took.

"I'm sorry you think of me that way, Vilstair, but I threw out every copy of the virus. It's gone. Maybe this will convince you."

He smiled and let his attention wander. He found Bakigan as the *Otteran* flew closer to the building. Vilstair had asked the Thlist police to help her against Madrigan and the others in the building, but she'd said nothing about the *Otteran*. She hadn't thought the ship mattered as much. Since they were lazy and since Geffin had paid them so much, none of the Thlist authorities tried to stop the *Otteran*.

Bakigan brought the *Otteran* in slowly, until it hovered beside the edge of the roof. The lift pinged as it reached the top, and the robots disgorged from it, each bearing an unconscious crew member. Bakigan blinked in bafflement, but lowered the ramp on the side of the *Otteran*. One by one, the robots trundled up the ramp, deposited their burden inside, and headed back. Loddrin's head hit the floor of the ship with an audible clang, but otherwise, everyone looked fine.

Once the last robot had cleared the ramp, Bakigan pulled it back, the door closing. The *Otteran* slid away from the building and rose high into the sky.

On the first floor of the building, the local police finally arrived. The newly-conscious guard met them outside his office, where he asked if he could please finally turn off the terrible music. When the police said he could, he slumped in grateful exhaustion. Looking amused and still in no rush, the police headed to the lifts. Since the robots were hogging them all, they had to wait.

The *Otteran* escaped Thlist's atmosphere. Bakigan entered coordinates for Darestacane, Polf's homeworld. When the ship reached the minimum safe distance, it jumped into hyperspace.

A few seconds later, a Gray frigate appeared on the other side of the system, a strike team on board. Three saireishi lurked on the ship. Madrigan fled from their minds.

He returned to himself to see that Vilstair had her blaster pointed at him again. It had been pointed at the floor when he last noticed it. So much sweat coated her that it looked like she'd been swimming. She gave a wide, triumphant grin as her finger finally pulled the trigger.

Madrigan didn't fight the stun, as he had the previous one. Geffin and the others were safe, and the galaxy knew the horrors that had occurred on Hreckin. That was all he needed. No matter what happened next, even torture or death, Madrigan wouldn't complain.

He collapsed to the floor with a smile on his face.

17

"Took you long enough," Vilstair said when the local police finally arrived. Gray gods, had they crawled all the way here?

She pressed a hand to her forehead, for all the good it would do. It would take at least four showers and changes of clothes before she felt clean and dry again.

"Where are the others?" one man asked. By the stripes on the side of his jacket, he was a sergeant.

"Escaped." Vilstair repressed the sneer or at least tried to. "Gray gods know where they went."

A ping came as a channel opened. Vilstair tapped her jewel to answer. She didn't look away as the local police snapped cuffs on Madrigan's wrists. Handcuffs wouldn't stop him, but it was better than nothing. Even though she'd shot him less than a minute ago, Vilstair stunned him again. He wasn't going to wake up again. Not anytime soon.

A middlesex Jrikshon appeared before her eyes, projected so only she could see. "Officer Bila, this is the Eckritun. What is the situation on Thlist?"

It was the Gray strike team — or *a* Gray strike team. According to her jewel, the Eckritun just came out of hyperspace. That meant she still didn't know what had happened to the previous strike team.

"Sergeant," she said, noting the bars on the Jrikshon's shoulder, "the saireishi Madrigan Farovan is unconscious.

The remaining members of the *Otteran* crew, including Geffin Chardan, escaped into hyperspace."

"I know. We missed them by less than a minute." The sergeant didn't look pleased by that. They narrowed their eyes and bared sharp teeth. "We found the strike team which came here before us. Everyone on board is asleep, but no one was injured. Since you say the situation is secure, we will stop to assist them, then meet you. Do not move, and stun Farovan every minute."

"With pleasure, sir."

The channel closed, with a final message that she should expect the team from the Eckritun in five minutes. That was far more efficient than the Thlist police. Considering how slow the locals were — a sloth that had doubtless been influenced by Chardan — that didn't say much. Still, it was faster than expected.

The Eckritun must hold one of the best teams from Diresi.

Vilstair itched to look into their record. It would surely overwhelm her — unless most of it was confidential. That would tell her things too.

She forced the curiosity away, focused instead on Farovan. He let her knock him out. She knew that, and she didn't like it. The last time he was knocked out, he woke far too soon. He might again wake quickly. He was a powerful saireishi. The Gray gods knew what he might have done to enhance himself.

Her jewel said that a minute had gone by since she had last stunned him, so she stunned him again. One of the Thlist police gave her a look, which she ignored. They could be offended as much as they wanted. Even if the sergeant hadn't ordered her to keep stunning Farovan, she would have done so anyway.

When a gasp came from her right, Vilstair shifted her

stance. She couldn't look away from Farovan, but she wanted to see Shinead.

Her new partner leaned heavily against the man helping her out of her restraints. From the way she blinked rapidly and didn't focus on anything, she must have just regained consciousness.

In the next chair, Butler muttered curses as he woke. Joranran laid on the floor, still asleep from the gas. A woman fluttered around him while administering him with a stimulant.

"Shinead? How are you?"

"Vilstair?" Shinead shook herself. The movement nearly made her fall sideways out of the chair. The man caught her and didn't let go until she looked steady. "You're free?" Shinead finally looked around the room. "It's over?"

Vilstair nodded. "Chardan and most of the *Otteran* crew got away." There hadn't been as many of the crew as there should have been. Perhaps most of them had been waiting on the ship. Vilstair didn't know.

Without Farovan, Chardan and his crew would fear capture. If they had any intelligence, they would make at least half a dozen jumps through hyperspace, ruining any chance of being followed. They would probably find a new world, preferably a mostly lawless one on the Neutral-Dark border, and keep their heads low for a while. Without Farovan, at least they weren't as dangerous.

Shinead stood with a groan. She walked slowly around the edge of the room, keeping one hand on the wall. Vilstair stunned Farovan a few times while she waited. Butler stood too, though he stayed quiet. He kept an eye on Joranran, who was loudly starting to come around, and Vilstair wondered what he would do next.

Five minutes after her conversation ended with the Eckritun, a group of people dressed in gray entered the room.

Their uniforms had a different cut than Vilstair and Shinead's: looser around the joints, thicker around the torso. Vilstair and Shinead were operatives who worked mostly independently. These were members of the Gray military, and the local police scowled at their proximity.

The Jrikshon sergeant stepped over to Vilstair and Shinead. "We'll take over. You may leave now."

A Gracknaren and a Kritilem moved closer to Farovan, standing on opposite sides. They didn't move, but stared down at him, barely blinking. A shiver ran down Vilstair's spine: those two were saireishi.

"What will happen to him?" The question came out before Vilstair thought to stop it.

Beside her, Shinead cringed. She tugged at Vilstair's arm. "Sorry, sir. We'll go now."

Vilstair refused to move. Maybe she shouldn't have asked the question, but she wanted to know. Farovan was barely more than a kid. The gods knew what sort of horrors he'd lived through. He inferred a few, and Vilstair didn't want to know enough to guess at more. What little she did know was already too much.

He was a criminal, but surely extenuating circumstances had to be taken into account. He'd been treated worse than an animal while growing up. As soon as he won his freedom, he fell into Chardan's company. That would mess anyone up.

"We will take him to Diresi." The sergeant stared at Farovan as they would a shiny new, but still untested, weapon. "There has never been an Ill-gotten saireishi before, Officer Bila. Neither has there been an unaligned saireishi. The Admirals will decide his fate."

Vilstair nodded. The Admirals were fair. She could only hope that Farovan wouldn't be killed. The Gray tried to avoid the death penalty, save when the Admirals and the populace listened to closely to Death's worshipers.

She hoped too that Farovan wouldn't be given life in a Gray prison. Perhaps he deserved it, but surely he'd already spent too much of his life in a cell.

Assuming there was a cell strong enough to hold him.

Probably the Admirals would offer to let him work as a Gray saireishi. If Farovan had any sense, he'd agree. The Gray would be firm while he was in training and until they were sure of his allegiance. The Gray was never cruel, though. It was the best ending for both the Gray and for Farovan.

With one last prayer to the Gray gods, Vilstair saluted the sergeant and allowed Shinead to lead her from the room.

* * *

The *Nebula's Edge* waited where they had left it, what felt like days ago. However beautiful Thlist was, Vilstair was ready to leave the planet.

It had only been five days since Writhim died. The realization made Vilstair cringe. When she checked her jewel, she saw that his memorial service had been moved back three times. It was scheduled to start in a few hours, in the morning in Diresi's capital.

It would take hours to reach Diresi, but she could probably make the end of the memorial. It would be enough to extend her condolences to his family. They deserved to hear about his death from someone who had been there.

"Do you want to go home?" she asked Shinead as they approached her ship.

Shinead had been quiet the entire trip. "Don't we have another mission?"

Vilstair hadn't checked in with Yafan. "I'm due a few days of leave." Her leave should have started days ago when Writhim died. It kept getting pushed back, one more delay and incident at a time. Vilstair wondered if Writhim's memorial had been moved back to accommodate her. Maybe not, but now she had to go.

"We fought a saireishi. We can take vacation time if someone complains. And I suppose we should take the time to get to know one another." Shinead wouldn't look at her.

"That sounds good." When Vilstair tapped her jewel, the ship's door opened, the ramp lowering. They hadn't taken anything off the ship save their weapons. When Vilstair spied Joranran and Butler's luggage, she frowned. With a shrug, she grabbed it and left it outside. They could come collect it if they wanted it.

As she was placing the last bag down, a voice called out, "Were you even planning to call us?"

Vilstair looked up to see Butler approach. Like her and Shinead, he'd taken a police vehicle to get here. As he climbed out of the hovervan, Vilstair saw no sign of Joranran.

"Of course I was going to call," she said, though she hadn't planned to. Both Joranran and Butler knew where the *Nebula's Edge* had been parked. That was the first place they'd check for their luggage. Thlist didn't see much theft, so it would wait for them here.

Butler snorted, tossing his horn into the air. "Are you going back to Diresi?"

"For a few days, yes." Shinead lingered a few steps behind Vilstair, inside the ship's door. She leaned against it, arms crossed over her chest, frown still in place.

"Do you need a ride?" Vilstair asked Butler.

He sighed. "Was it that obvious? Being Jorn has no money. Even if I wanted to work for him — and I don't — he can't afford me. In fact, he's in debt to me since I only take half my commission in advance. Considering that he's likely to end up in jail, I don't expect I'll be paid anytime soon. Do you mind if I come with you? There's always work on Diresi."

Throughout their time together, Vilstair never asked Butler how he felt about Ill-gotten. He seemed to have no problems with her, so she had assumed he wasn't an asshole. It pleased her that he'd left Joranran behind, and that Joranran would get what he deserved. "There's plenty of room," she said, moving aside.

Butler grabbed his two bags and climbed on. When he saw her staring at Joranran's luggage, he smirked and said, "Maybe let me tell him. If he hears from you, he might start wibbling again. When you left without him, he started to cry."

"Gray gods." Vilstair closed her eyes for a moment. "The Gray saireishi didn't fix his brain?"

"No. I think they were amused by it."

"Gray gods fuck it. I am not calling him!" She strode into the cockpit without waiting for Butler's response. Shinead finally smiled, and that made Vilstair feel a little better. She kept complaining about Joranran. By the time the *Nebula's Edge* jumped into hyperspace, Shinead was laughing.

It hadn't been a bad five days, Vilstair decided as she climbed into her narrow bunk, hoping to finally get some quality sleep. She had lost a friend, but she'd gained a new one. Maybe two, if she counted Butler. She'd stopped a powerful saireishi on her own, helped bring justice to Hreckin, and saved the lives of countless Ill-gotten.

As she drifted off to sleep, she made a mental note to delete all her copies of Joranran's holocins. They no longer held any appeal to her. Writhim hated those films: he always had good taste.

18

"Where is the virus?"

The words thundered through Madrigan's head. He drifted, caught somewhere between waking and sleep. Three minds pressed down on his.

He had never fought against a saireishi before. On Hreckin, the scientists kept the children separate, afraid they would work together. Madrigan had a plan for how he would attack a mind like his, but it was only guesswork.

The minds pushed down on him, trying to smother him between them. Madrigan pictured himself in a room with fortified walls, strong enough to resist anything. He sat in the middle of his imagined room, his knees drawn up against his chest. He didn't really sit, though — he could feel his body, distant, lying down and restrained.

"Where is the virus?" The words came again, stronger than the last time.

"I told Vilstair. It's gone."

Fire raged beyond his safe room. The flames licked the walls but couldn't get past.

When the fire couldn't get past, a terrible wind blew through. It howled at the walls, strove to push them down. Madrigan didn't flinch. He had seen far worse than this. No wind would tear down his walls.

The flood came next. The enemy saireishi swam through his outer consciousness, throwing up waves and tossing everything around. They took away the ground that his room sat upon. Water rushed down from above, trying to drown him.

The floor and ceiling were as strong as the walls. Madrigan was no fool.

"The virus is gone," he said, louder this time, willing the saireishi to hear him. The waves calmed somewhat.

"It cannot be gone."

"It is. I checked. The scientists never gave out copies of the virus, not even the directions on how to make the virus. They had only a few samples. The Hreckin government wanted them to put the virus into production, but they refused." It wasn't mercy that kept the scientists from making copies of the virus. They found Ill-gottens more useful as captives.

"Koryan Jorn had copies."

Madrigan shook his head. "He funded the lab, so that's where his copy came from. He had a pill-version, not something air-borne. It's a weaker version. The scientists would never give him the real version. The original is gone, I promise."

The water churned in one direction, faster and faster. It tried to suck down his room. Madrigan let it take him. It didn't matter where his room ended up. So long as he stayed strong, the saireishi wouldn't reach him.

"You took a copy."

He had. He found a canister in the hallway of the laboratory on his way out. A month after leaving Hreckin, he took a ship deep into hyperspace, near the edge of the galaxy, in the disputed zone. There was a group of quasars there, some of the brightest and hottest stars in the galaxy. His ship had a small escape pod, one with a hyperdrive engine. The engine wouldn't go far, but he didn't need it to go far.

Madrigan put the canister on the escape shuttle,

programmed its hyperdrive, and let the shuttle go. It jumped away from his ship and ended up in the heart of the quasar in the middle of the cluster.

"I told you, it's gone." He held up those memories, forming a brief window in his room. The images slipped through in an instant, and the window vanished after, once more becoming a strong wall that nothing could break through.

The voices stayed silent for a time as they considered the memories. Madrigan wasn't sure how much time elapsed. Adrift from his body and his outer consciousness, he couldn't judge time.

He didn't mind the silence. Water still thrashed about his room, but only enough to remind him of the threat, only enough to require his constant attention to keep it at bay. On Hreckin, the scientists sometimes tested Madrigan for hours. He could keep this up as long as he needed to.

"You know how the virus was made."

The voices came back suddenly, and the water stopped around him. No wind or fire replaced it. Everything was silent around Madrigan.

"I don't."

"You do. Your jewel took readings of the canister and the virus. You had to ensure it was as dangerous as you believed."

"I did. I put that jewel on the same escape pod as the virus. I know nothing about making viruses. I don't remember."

Laughter came. It bounced off the walls of his room. Fire, wind, and water hadn't made Madrigan shudder, but the laughter did. He knew that laughter. He heard it many times in his youth from the scientists. That laugh meant confidence and cruelty. It meant a determination that would not accept failure.

"You don't remember, but the information is in your mind, buried deep. There are other things you know. You have forgotten them now, but you will remember. We will make you remember."

"Oh." Madrigan released his knees. His legs splayed before him.

He hadn't thought about that. He had never reached that deep into a person's mind before, but the scientists said it could be done. They'd heard reports about such power in other saireishi. As far as Madrigan knew, none of the other children on Hreckin ever managed such a feat.

His training had been the result of a hundred years of guesswork. The scientists only had a vague idea of how sairei worked. The various cabals of saireishi kept that secret. While Madrigan and the other children got very good at the bits the scientists could figure out, far more remained a mystery.

Until now, Madrigan thought maybe a saireishi couldn't read something a person had forgotten. It seemed he was wrong.

"Is it going to hurt?" he asked. His room was secure for now, but for how long? He was a captive of the Gray. They could spend weeks, months, or years breaking into his mind. It didn't matter how powerful he was. Eventually, they would wear him down. Especially if they started to hurt his body. Madrigan drifted away from it at the moment, but they could drag him closer.

"Only if you resist."

Madrigan shook his head. "Why do you want to know? The Gray is supposed to love Ill-gotten. I've forgotten. If you let it stay forgotten, no one will ever know."

"Fate requires it."

That made Madrigan frown. He knew some of Gray politics, more than most non-Gray paths would know. Fate was the strongest of the Gray gods, the one who held the

Gray alliance together. It was said that Fate was the strongest of all the gods, except the Destroyer.

"Are the Ill-gotten fated to be wiped out from existence?" The Gray shouldn't want such a thing. Fate was mysterious, but he was supposed to love his worshipers. Surely he had Ill-gotten amongst his followers.

"What Fate wants is not your concern. Submit, and you will be spared."

Madrigan smiled. He thought of Geffin, Polf, Loddrin, Bakigan, and the other members of the *Otteran* crew. They were safe now, somewhere far away. He thought of Vilstair, so fierce. She could have killed him; maybe she should have. She hadn't. In the end, he had caught compassion and understanding from her mind.

If Madrigan submitted, his friends would be in danger. If Madrigan lost, Vilstair would die. Placed against that, his own life meant very little.

He laid on the ground. Because it only existed in his mind, it was soft under his back. He smiled and wiggled about, getting comfortable.

"If Fate wants to kill all the Ill-gotten, then I will fight Fate."

"No one fights Fate."

Madrigan laughed. "No one escaped the lab before me. I think I'll take my chances."

The space outside shifted, and Madrigan could feel his body again. Pain rushed over him. He kept smiling. He knew what he had to do, and he wasn't afraid.

With no danger in his mind, he let the room around him weaken. He didn't lose it entirely because he needed protection, where he was going.

He plunged deeper into his own mind. The voices, thinking he did so to avoid the pain of his body, let him go. They didn't know him, and they didn't know what he had planned.

The scientists on Hreckin could only learn sairei by experiment and observation, but they learned a few things. They learned early on how easy it was to kill a person from inside the mind. A saireishi only needed to find the right place and push in the right way. Madrigan had killed people that way.

He reached the depths of his mind. A soft spot waited there. Darkness loomed beyond it: a curtain, beyond which death waited. Madrigan was Neutral, so he'd end up in Death's underworld. The dead always mourned when they first stepped through the gates into the underworld, but eventually they found happiness. So all the priests said, and so Madrigan believed.

One day, hopefully a long time in the future, Geffin, Vilstair, and everyone else he loved would die. Geffin was Neutral, and Vilstair was Gray. They too would spend eternity in the infinite plains of the underworld. Madrigan could wait for them to arrive.

With one last smile, he pushed the soft spot in his mind. The curtain parted, and Madrigan stepped through.

Madrigan is dead.

I couldn't save him. Yonaven forced me to practice, to spend all my time and energy on Gratevon, where she knows I can't function properly. She kept me busy while the Gray attacked Madrigan, and now it's too late.

I try to reach him anyway. I couldn't save him, couldn't rescue him from the Gray, but maybe I can do something. Maybe I'm not too late. The Gray wants things from him: information and power. Until they get it, they'll keep him alive.

That's what I thought, but the Gray is far more terrible than anyone has realized. Even I, who have suffered more under the Gray than anyone else, didn't realize the Gray could do this.

Madrigan knew what had happened to him. He knew the Gray wanted things from him, things he refused to give them. Their saireishi held him in their power. He's stronger than any of their saireishi, but he was outnumbered. They had all the time they needed. Madrigan realized that. To protect his secrets, to protect Geffin and his other friends, and to protect me — he doesn't know about me, doesn't know that I survived Hreckin, but he wants to protect me anyway. That's the kind of person he is.

The kind of person he was.

He's dead. He killed himself. He turned his power inward and shut down his brain. It's something any saireishi of decent power and skill can do. He did it to protect others, and he wasn't afraid.

What am I supposed to do now? Madrigan was the only person I loved, the only person who ever did anything for me. He's gone, but I remain.

I could follow his lead. If I closed my eyes and looked, I could find the special place in my own mind. I could die. Yonaven watches often, but not all the time. If I'm patient and wait for the right chance, I could die.

I don't want to die. I've never lived, not really. My life has been constant suffering. I can only watch, changing nothing. There would be joy in death, eventually.

I want to go to Madrigan, and I want to find joy, but I don't want to die.

So, what should I do?

I don't know. For the first time in my life, I'm lost. That terrifies me more than anything else.

In the end, I do what I always do. I watch. That's all I can do.

Afterward

N E Riggs is from Chicago and currently lives in Vincennes, Indiana. N E is a math professor and martial artist who likes to combine fantasy and science fiction elements in new and weird ways.

<u>NERiggs.com</u>

For a free anthology go to:
<u>NERiggs.com/signup</u>

Sorcery, Spaceships, & Sarcasm

Shadows of an Empire:
Swift as the Wind

Only the Inevitable:
The Antlions of Vanlang

A More Efficient Fantasy:
Optimizing Evil

Thousand Eye Universe:
Chasing Relics